BETRAYED

Joe Wolfkiller tossed his blanket aside and rose, drawing his pistol at the same moment. John Berg simultaneously threw his own blanket aside, exposing a sawed-off Greener shotgun to the red glow of the fire.

"That's enough stirring around right there, Cherokee Joe," Berg said. "You ain't going nowhere but to Arkansas."

At the same time, Little and Pease also came awake—if they had ever really been asleep at all—and threw aside their own blankets to expose drawn weapons. Pease had a pistol, Little a shotgun that was twin to the one Berg held.

"Drop that pistol, half-breed," Berg ordered.

Joe looked around from face to face. All were featureless in the fading red fireglow. He sighed loudly, then let his pistol fall to the ground.

Pease chuckled and stepped forward. Berg and Little lowered their shotguns and did the same, all eager to be the first to officially lay hand on the much-wanted Cherokee Joe, now a prisoner of Parker's court.

Joe Wolfkiller dropped with the speed of a stone. He landed flat on his stomach, sweeping up the pistol he had let fall. Little raised his shotgun and fired. . . .

CHEROKEE JOE

Cameron Judd

BANTAM BOOKS
NEW YORK · TORONTO · LONDON · SYDNEY · AUCKLAND

CHEROKEE JOE
A Bantam Domain Book / March 1992

ISBN 0-553-29420-2

Published simultaneously in the United States and Canada

Bantam Books are published by Bantam Books, a division of
Bantam Doubleday Dell Publishing Group, Inc. Its trademark,
consisting of the words "Bantam Books" and the portrayal of a
rooster, is Registered in U.S. Patent and Trademark Office and
in other countries. Marca Registrada. Bantam Books, 666 Fifth
Avenue, New York, New York 10103.

PRINTED IN THE UNITED STATES OF AMERICA

RAD   0 9 8 7 6 5 4 3 2 1

For Denise, sister and supporter

CHEROKEE JOE

Chapter 1

The hog charged and rammed its victim for the ninth time just as another .44 slug ripped through the shed wall. Joe Wolfkiller, a swarthy young man with long black hair and broad, high cheekbones sculpted by the Cherokee half of his ancestry, grimaced and thrust his face down into the mucky straw in which he lay. Splinters and grit from the punctured wall rained down around him. The hog retreated, squealed, charged a tenth time, then withdrew to the rear of the bullet-riddled shed, grunting and slobbering.

Slowly Joe Wolfkiller lifted his head, his face dappled with mud and manure and whiskered with straw. He lay behind a heavy foundation beam about ten inches high, the only piece of wood in the shed thick enough to protect him from the bullets sporadically spat toward him from the tiny house across the clearing. Cautiously he peered through a knothole toward that house.

Smoke drifted around a north-facing window. He saw movement behind the broken glass and thought of rolling closer to the shed door so that he could return fire from it, but the impulse was fleeting. Joe Wolfkiller, for once in his life, didn't want to fight, just get away. His antagonist, a usually harmless potbellied no-account named Hambone Coltrane, was not a man he wished to harm. In fact, Joe was used to thinking of Coltrane as a friend, or at least one of the closest facsimiles he had known in a largely friendless experience. Only when Coltrane was drunk and dejected, as now, did he turn sour and threatening, though never before had he tried to gun down his companion.

1

Behind Joe, the hog grunted loudly and sank into the reeking moist straw. Joe glanced back; tiny bloodshot eyes glared at him, full of fear and an animalistic approximation of hate.

Coltrane's voice came from the house. "You dead yet, Joe? You dead yet?"

Joe Wolfkiller put his mouth close to the knothole and shouted back. "Not dead—but this hog will be if you keep shooting!"

No answer. Silence hung heavy. Some instinct warned Joe, and he buried his face in the filth again, digging deep as another shot blasted the knothole into a ragged gash and passed through the shed to nick the hog's left ear.

The beast rose, squealing in pain, and charged Joe again. This time it bit him on the calf, jerking its head from side to side like a wolf trying to rip meat from a fresh kill. Joe let out a yell as he tugged free.

"Got ya that time, Joe—gotya!" Coltrane shouted triumphantly, misinterpreting the meaning of Joe's yell.

Joe had no time to answer, for the hog was on him again, ramming and grunting porcine threats. Joe could take no more. He rolled onto his back, aimed his mud-grimed Colt, and squeezed the trigger. The bullet took instant effect. The hog's pink eyes widened and dulled. It fell heavily to the side, a little rivulet of blood flowing from the bullet hole between and slightly above its eyes.

Joe rolled to the left and lay staring at the animal. Maybe he shouldn't have killed it, he thought. Now Hambone really would be furious. He had always loved that hog.

"Joe?" Coltrane sounded uncertain. He had heard Joe's shot. "What'd you do just then, Joe?"

Joe wiped his pistol on his denim trousers. "Killed your hog, Hambone," he yelled through the wall.

A pause. "What'd you say, Joe?"

"I said I killed your hog."

In a moment a great muffled wail of grief reached Joe's ears. He dug himself into the mud floor again, knowing what would follow.

This time Coltrane fired three shots in quick succession, puncturing a wallboard with the first two and knocking it clean out with the third. Still vibrating, it fell back on the dead hog. As the noise of the gunfire echoed away, Joe heard Coltrane cursing in a voice hoarse with weeping.

Joe rolled back to the right, then heaved up and over the dead hog, using its warm mass for cover. Peering over its side, he eyed Coltrane's tiny house through the gap where the wall plank had been. He looked for Coltrane behind his window and did not see him.

A moment later the house's single door opened, and Coltrane came dashing out, carrying his smoking rifle, his ample belly jiggling as he ran toward the roughly built stable diagonally across the clearing. Coltrane wore galluses but no shirt. His greasy trousers rode so low that the upper part of his buttocks pooched above the baggy seat.

Joe recognized his opportunity to shoot his foe but did not take it. He still had no desire to harm Coltrane, and he felt guilty about killing Coltrane's beloved hog. It was a novel feeling. Joe Wolfkiller seldom felt guilty about anything.

"I'm sorry about the hog!" Joe yelled at the running man. "It was trying to eat my leg off."

By now, Coltrane had reached the stable. Joe wondered if Coltrane planned to go around the stable and approach the hog shed from the side or rear. That theory was shattered by a shot from inside the stable. A terrible trumpeting whinny followed, then a dead thud.

With a burst of horror, Joe realized what Coltrane had just done. "You shot my horse, Hambone!" Joe yelled.

"It was fair—you kilt my hog!" Coltrane yelled back. "You had no call to kill my hog!"

Joe, fiercely angry, raised his pistol and impulsively fired a shot through the stable. Immediately he wished he hadn't. "Hambone! You all right?"

Hambone Coltrane, obviously unscathed, emerged from the stable and pounded heavily back to the house. Joe lowered himself behind the dead hog, wondering how long this foolish standoff would continue.

For a long time there was no sound except the wind and wails from the house as Hambone grieved over his hog. Joe thought about Coltrane's slaughter of his horse and became more philosophical about it. The horse hadn't been hard to come by, after all. He had stolen it, and its saddle too, a month before. His biggest regret was that now the horse was dead, he had no good means of escape. There was always Hambone's mount, of course, but that was nothing but a balky mule whose fastest clip was a weary lope.

Joe thought about kicking out a rear-wall plank, squeezing through to freedom, and making a run on foot, but he feared Coltrane would come after him, which could only result in his having to shoot Hambone, or vice versa.

So he just lay there, hiding behind the dead hog. Minutes passed. The day waned, and the March air began to cool, the hog cooling along with it. Joe watched shadows outside stretch east toward Missouri, growing longer and darker as the sun traveled westward and down. A gopher skittered across the clearing. Joe began to feel tired.

Hambone Coltrane's curses and moans became softer and less frequent. Joe watched the window carefully for signs of Coltrane repositioning himself to shoot again. Every now and then he would see Coltrane's face look out, but no shooting followed. Finally, as dusk came, Joe concluded that Coltrane had gotten over his anger, or maybe had drunk himself into a stupor.

Standing inside the shed, keeping his eye on the house, Joe stretched his stiff legs and moved his body from side to side. All the filth that covered him had now dried to a thick crust that stiffened his pants and long dark coat and scabbed his skin. He longed for a good wash.

Softly, Joe walked to the door of the shed. Still watching the house, he stepped into the dusty clearing. Noiseless and light as cattail fluff in the wind, he crossed to the stable. His horse was dead, as Coltrane had said. Joe looked at it regretfully. At least he still had the saddle, which lay on its side in the corner of the stable. He picked up the saddle and heaved it onto his shoulder.

Joe was sure now that Coltrane was asleep or passed out, so he grew less cautious. He was surprised when the door opened and Hambone Coltrane came staggering out. Joe dropped the saddle and drew his pistol. Coltrane came right on toward him, carrying something. Joe saw it was his saddlebags, which he had taken into the house prior to the card game that had led to this altercation in the first place.

"I seen you leaving, Joe," Coltrane slurred, sounding meek as a puppy now. "I knew you'd want these here bags." Coltrane's face, from what Joe could see in the early-evening darkness, was puffy and red, his eyes swollen from drinking and crying about the hog. Coltrane glanced down at the pistol in Joe's hand. "You don't need that, Joe. I don't want no more trouble with you."

"You wanted plenty of it before," said Joe, keeping the pistol right where it was.

"I know, and I'm mighty sorry." Coltrane had put on a shirt sometime before and swiped the crusty sleeve of the left arm under his rheumy nose. "I didn't never want to hurt you. Not really."

"Drop the saddlebags and move over yonder," Joe said. "And keep where I can see you."

"Joe, don't treat me so. You got nothing to worry over from me."

"You gave me plenty to worry over in that hog shed. And you killed my horse."

Coltrane sniffed again. "I was wrong to do it. I admit it." A tear rolled down his face.

Joe was repulsed. He disliked drunks and trusted them less, and Coltrane was proving to be that particularly unstable kind who swing from mean to maudlin. Joe figured he could just as easily swing back to mean again. The last thought made Joe realize how unwise it would be to set out on foot, leaving Coltrane with a mount. The man might turn on him again and try to chase him down in the dark. "I'm taking your mule," Joe announced.

Coltrane nodded as if he had expected nothing else. "It's fair payment for what I done, I reckon."

"Payment, but not fair payment. The horse you shot was worth a lot more than that mule," Joe replied sourly. He felt wronged; it was his way to take bitter note of wrongs done him, overlooking those wrongs he did to others. At the moment he had all but forgotten that the slain horse was never honestly his to begin with.

"I'm a sorry old soul, Joe. I've always knowed I was,"

Hambone blubbered, almost ready to cry again. "You was right to shoot my hog, just to punish me for the way I done you."

"I shot it to keep it from taking a bite out of me, that's all. You can get some meat off it at least." Joe holstered his pistol and went to the stable. He led out the mule and began saddling it.

"Can't bring myself to eat that hog," Coltrane said. "My Maudie loved it since it was just a little pink thing. Treated it like a house pup that winter she died. Ever since I laid her away, that hog's always put me in mind of Maudie" He choked as a sob welled up.

Joe Wolfkiller had no time to listen to a grown man crying over a dead hog or a dead wife. He finished his saddling and mounted. The mule, not used to so light a rider, moved its ears and seemed bewildered. After some goading, the mule began to step forward. Joe kept Coltrane in the corner of his eye, just in case he had a pistol hidden on him and had done all this to get an opportunity to shoot on the sneak.

He didn't. His fleshy figure looked rather pitiful there in the darkening clearing. "Goodbye, Cherokee Joe," Coltrane said as Joe went out of sight in the dark.

Joe Wolfkiller made no reply. The mule plodded along through the thickening Kansas night as the wind grew more chilly.

It was by the name Cherokee Joe that the twenty-two-year-old halfbreed named Joe Wolfkiller was best known in the Indian Territory and up into Kansas. He had never been particularly fond of the nickname, but he was proud of the growing infamy attached to it.

Joe had known from childhood that a life of trouble lay before him. He had been able to smell it coming, as a good hunter could smell a deer or buffalo. His father, a full-blood Cherokee named Sam Wolfkiller who raised Joe alone after his white mother died giving him birth, had also foreseen his son's destiny and worried over it. Sometimes young Joe had been able to see his father's concerns reflected like the firelight in the deep black of his eyes. Such visions had never disturbed Joe. If strife was to be his lot, let it be. He would not run from it. He would drink deeply of it, slake his greatest thirsts on it, thrive from it.

Such an attitude, predictably, had made Joe's anticipations and Sam Wolfkiller's worries self-fulfilling. Before he was into his teens, Joe Wolfkiller was known as a fighter and troublemaker among his peers in the Cherokee Nation of the Indian Territory. Before he was twenty, he was suspected in a string of thefts and beatings. One of the latter had proved nearly fatal to the victim. To the chagrin of the law and many of the Cherokees there was never enough evidence to prove Joe's guilt, though no one doubted it.

The authorities had thereafter kept a close eye on the halfbreed whom the soldiers at Fort Gibson began calling Cherokee Joe. The fact that he was neither fully Indian nor fully white was enough to make many distrust him. That he was prone to violence made him unlikable as well. The older he grew, the more Cherokee Joe found himself at odds with the world around him. Gradually he grew bitter and in an odd, paradoxical way, found his bitterness sweet. It gave him a rationale for breaking any rules he wanted to break and a justification for coddling the hatred and anger that drove him.

Joe had been on the run for many months now, living by his wits on the grasslands of Kansas, making or taking a living however he could. It had been a new accusation of crime that drove him from his home near Tahlequah. The charge was attempted murder, the victim a troublesome roughneck who had tangled with Joe several times. Now the roughneck would do nothing for the rest of his days but sit silently in a chair, staring and drooling.

But this time Joe was innocent. The man who had administered the beating was the outlaw Caul Slidell, whose gang Joe had ridden with on occasion. Slidell, like many of his ilk, frequently hid out along the rivers and ravines of the Indian Territory. He had never liked Cherokee Joe enough to let him affiliate fully with his select band of hellriders, as he called them. Joe suspected that Slidell had deliberately set him up to look guilty.

The mule plodded through the darkness. Joe's belly

was empty and grumbling, but he had no food. He swore at himself for not having thought to take food from Coltrane.

At last a distant sparkle of light off to the west caught Joe's eye. He knew the source. It was the lantern hanging out front of Shadrah Camp's Boardinghouse and Restaurant, which, along with a handful of houses, stood beside a livery stable and mercantile store where two dirt roads crossed. Joe was tempted to make for the light. It meant food, a bath, shelter, maybe a game of cards. Countering the temptation was the fact that he had little money and could easily run in to the law or some other trouble at a public stop like Camp's.

He halted the mule, weighed his options, and temptation overruled prudence. He justified the decision with the thought that maybe at the little community he could find a way to replace Coltrane's mule, by trade or theft, with a more worthy mount. He called the mule a foul name and goaded it forward. The flicker of light grew brighter and closer, and when Joe was near enough to catch a whiff of beef stew wafting out of the café, he was as trapped as a sailor hearing the song of Sirens.

Joe hitched the mule, then paused at the window of the café and examined its occupants before going to the door. He recognized no one. The door was homemade of rough lumber but beautified somewhat by a pane of red-and-white-checkered glass. Joe paused to gather his long hair in his hand and tuck it up under his wide-brimmed hat. In his youth, the teachers at the Indian Agency school had made him cut his hair short. Now he wore it long in defiance of them and their world. But when a man's belly is empty, Joe had learned, sometimes it's best to put defiance aside long enough to find a meal.

The door creaked as it opened, and everyone inside turned to watch Joe enter. From the lifting of brows and the subtle movements of the corners of mouths, Joe knew he was rousing interest. Proprietor Shadrah Camp, a beefy man in armbands and an apron, wiped his fingers on a towel and stepped up to him, lowering heavy brows, the only hair on him from the neck up.

Camp's flyspeck eyes looked Joe up and down. "You

can't come in here all filthied up like that, boy," Camp said. "Take you a wash at that trough yonder if you want in here."

Joe held Camp's gaze a few seconds, then turned so abruptly that Camp was startled into a backstep. Joe heard the patrons inside give a titter of laughter at Camp's reaction.

Ignoring the cool air, Joe stripped off his jacket and shirt at the trough and washed his skin in the dirty water. He washed his hair out, too, and let the wind dry it partially before he tucked it beneath the hat again. By now, the muck on his pants and shirt was dry enough to flake off; what remained he was able to remove partially by dabbing the dirtiest spots with trough water. When he was as clean as he could get, Joe dressed again and returned to the café.

This time Camp did not try to stop him, though he did glance down at Joe's hip, clearly wondering if there was a pistol under the long coat. He opted not to ask.

The meal, which cost Joe almost all his money, was salted ham, potatoes, biscuits, and coffee. Joe was halfway through with it when the glass-paned door opened again. When he saw the man who walked through it, he set his coffee cup down and reached for his pistol.

The newcomer was Tom Pease, and Joe knew him well.

Chapter 2

When he noticed Cherokee Joe, Pease gave no other reaction than a fleeting look of surprise, followed at once by a slight grin. Pease glanced at the row of pegs on the wall to his right; five gunbelts hung there, but there were six patrons in the room. Joe figured that Pease would have no problem deciding which of the six had not given up his weapon.

Pease took off his hat, revealing a closely cropped head of stiff brown hair. His eyes flickered to Joe another moment; then he looked away and walked to a corner table.

Joe Wolfkiller returned to his meal, but kept Pease in the corner of his eye. He watched as Pease sat down, laid his hat on the table before him, and placed his order with Shadrah Camp. While he waited for his coffee, Pease fiddled with the crow feather stuck into the band of the battered tan hat. When his coffee arrived, Pease turned slightly in his chair so that he faced Joe Wolfkiller more squarely. His eyes lifted and looked at those of the half-breed while he took his first sip. When the cup was lowered, Pease nodded slightly, his first open acknowledgment of Joe.

Joe did not return the gesture. His right hand was still under the table. Pease grinned again as he noted Joe's coolness, then shifted, looking away. Shortly after, Camp came in with a plate of eggs and bread.

As Camp turned away, Pease said, "Just a minute, friend," and stood, scooting back his chair.

10

Joe Wolfkiller watched cautiously now. Pease made a deliberate show of pulling back his coat and unbuckling the fine leather holster belt around his waist. He handed the belt, bearing a Remington pistol, to Shadrah Camp. "Hang it on them pegs for me until I go," he said. "That's the house rule, ain't it?"

"Yes, sir, it is," Camp replied. As he walked away with the gunbelt, he fired a quick glance toward Joe.

Pease sat down again and looked back at Joe, smiling openly and lifting his coffee cup in salute. Joe relaxed somewhat; he recognized Pease's relinquishing his pistol as an obvious message of nonaggression. Still he did not let his hand drift far from his side arm, for he knew from experience that Tom Pease was not to be trusted.

Pease gulped down his meal like a hungry dog, then wiped a checked napkin over his mouth. Joe remained at his table even though his meal was finished; he wanted to keep his eye on Pease. Something in Pease's manner suggested that this chance encounter would not pass without words, and Joe had to admit some curiosity about what Pease would have to say.

Pease stood, fished coins from his pocket, and laid them beside his plate. He picked up his hat and coffee and walked over to Joe's table.

Joe stared up at the tall, gangly man dressed in woolen trousers, a faded blue collarless shirt, checkered vest, and a long-tailed overjacket. Pease's soft leather boots reached up almost to his knees, the trousers tucked down into them.

"Howdy, Joe," Pease said quietly. "Mind if I have a seat?"

Joe's stare gave no permission, but no denial either. That was good enough for Pease. He pulled back the chair across from Joe's and sat. "Didn't expect to walk in here and find Cherokee Joe filling his gullet," Pease said.

"What do you want?" Joe Wolfkiller was always forthright.

"Just to talk to you," Pease said. "I'm glad to run into you—there's something you ought to know."

"Say what you've got to say."

"All right. It's about your father."

Joe Wolfkiller felt a prickle on the back of his neck. He had not been in contact with Sam Wolfkiller in months. A deep-rooted fear was that his father would come to harm, or the end of his life, with him far away.

Pease took another swallow of coffee and looked solemn. "Sam's in a poor way, Joe. He's bad sick, real bad."

Dread settled over Joe Wolfkiller. "How long?"

"Three weeks, maybe a month. He ain't long for this world, from what I hear. He's been calling for you to come back."

Joe's heart sped in his chest, though he presented no change of expression. He studied Pease's face, his eyes, looking for signs of deception. He found none. "I can't go back," Joe said. "There's trouble waiting for me in the Territory."

"It's your choice. Look, Joe, you and me have had our differences. I could have walked out of here and not told you about your father, and what little conscience I got left wouldn't have hurt me enough to make me scratch. I don't figure I owe you nothing. But I figure a man has a right to know when his father's calling for him."

"If I return to the Territory, I'll end up in Parker's jail."

"Not if you don't get caught, you won't."

Joe thought it over. A surge of uncomfortable heat was rising in his gut. He did not like to admit fear, even to himself, but the cold truth was that the prospect of returning to the Indian Territory frightened him. If it was common knowledge that Sam Wolfkiller was ill and calling for him, the law would be lying in wait for the son's return. Joe was ever mindful of the attempted-murder charge pending against him across the Territory border.

Pease resettled himself and gave Joe a sincere look. "Listen, Joe, I know it ain't my business, and you probably don't want me nowhere around, but by Satan's granny, if you want me to go with you, I will. I'll do whatever I can to let you see Sam and then get you safe out of the Territory again."

Now Joe Wolfkiller seemed to withdraw. A hard, impenetrable coldness frosted his small eyes. "Why should I trust you?" he said. "I know the man you are."

Pease fidgeted uncomfortably. "You got cause to feel that way, I admit. There ain't nothing I can tell you but I'm a better man now than I was when all that other happened. Besides, you paid me back fair and square. I hated you for it, but I know I got what I deserved."

Through Joe's mind played the memory of Pease's treachery. Two years ago it had been. He, Pease, and two others had broken into a reservation store by night and forced open its strongbox. They had been detected. Men had come, bearing badges and guns. There had been shooting. Pease deserted Joe in a narrow graveled wash, forcing him to shoot his way out only to find his horse gone. Pease had taken it to replace his own, which had thrown a shoe. Joe fled on foot, the darkness his only ally. Amazingly, he came through the encounter alive and uncaptured, swearing vengeance upon Tom Pease. He had achieved that vengeance shortly afterward, knifing Pease so badly he had almost died. Glancing down now at Pease's left hand, Joe noted the long scar across his palm, a vestige of a slash received as Pease tried to push away Joe's blade.

"I'm ready to put all our trouble behind, Joe," Pease said. "A man can't carry his grudges forever."

That was a novel notion for Joe Wolfkiller, who had never let a grudge go in his life. He wondered if Pease might be sincere.

Still faced by Joe's silent stare, Pease exhaled loudly. "Well, Joe, I can see this is over and done. I've done the right thing by telling you about Sam, and I'm ready to help you if you're willing. And if you're not, I'll just walk out of here and ride away."

Joe lowered his head a moment, then raised it again. "I'll go with you," he said. "But if you turn on me, Pease, this time my knife will cut out your heart."

"I won't turn on you. You'll see what I mean when I say I'm a better man. We'll ride out tomorrow."

"Tomorrow," said Joe Wolfkiller.

* * *

Joe had known little good fortune in his life and was surprised when some came his way the next morning. Pease eyed the recalcitrant mule Joe had been riding and declared it unsuitable for the long ride back to Joe's home in the Cherokee Nation. Shadrah Camp ran a few horses for trade in a lot a hundred yards behind the boarding house, and there Pease haggled, threw in a little cash, and replaced the mule with a quarterhorse that was old but somewhat better.

"It's yours, Joe," Pease said.

Camp, meanwhile, was taking a closer look at the mule he had just accepted as partial payment for the horse. "This looks like Hambone Coltrane's mule," he said.

"It was, until I won it on a fair wager," Joe replied.

Camp, still maintaining a cautious tread around the grim halfbreed, cast a suspicious glance but wisely said nothing.

"He's thinking you stole it," Pease side-whispered.

"Let him say it to my face," Joe replied coldly. "He'll regret it for the rest of a short life."

Pease wondered why Joe Wolfkiller was so offended at being thought a thief when he truly had been a thief so many times. Joe had always been hard for Pease to decipher.

They mounted and rode southeast. "I want to know why you were willing to give money to get me a horse," Joe said.

"Because I want you to know I mean it about making up for what's been wrong between us," Pease replied. "You can pay me back later, I figure."

Joe thought about it, feeling suspicious. Why was Pease here in Kansas to begin with? He had always stayed in Arkansas or around the railroad stations in the Indian Territory. Despite his doubts, Joe continued riding beside his sometime partner and sometime foe, carrying distrust like an unseen mantle over his shoulders.

By the time Joe and Pease were deep into the wide bluestem grasslands of the Flint Hills, Joe knew that Pease really had changed in one way, from taciturn to talkative.

As the miles dropped away behind them, Pease kept up a continual droning chatter, talking in his Arkansas brogue of the changes that were coming to the world Joe had known all his life. "Mark my words, the Indian Territory like we know it ain't long to be," Pease said. "Them Washington gents is getting ready to open the district up for settlers, and when they do, look out and stand aside! Satan's granny, Joe, when I rode up a week ago, there was already wagonloads of folk setting up camps all along the south Kansas border, just waiting for word to start their run. Give it a few more weeks, and you'll see thousands more joining them, snorting steam and ready to race."

"Those lands were promised by the United States to the Indians for as long as the rivers run," Joe commented. His words carried no passion. Joe had learned the futility of raging at the broken promises of the whites. Rage achieved nothing. Careful vengeance did.

"What the government gives, the government takes away." Pease had no more affection for the government than Joe. The son of an embittered Arkansas ex-Confederate, Pease kept alive his father's dark viewpoint on the conflict of the 1860s. "The Five Civilized Tribes ain't been forgave yet for siding with the South against the Yankee aggression."

Even so politically apathetic a fellow as Joe Wolfkiller understood the situation Pease referred to. The Five Civilized Tribes, consisting of the Choctaws, Cherokees, Creeks, Seminoles, and Chickasaws, had signed individual agreements after the outbreak of the Civil War to support the Confederacy. The Cherokees had been divided on the issue, but because many prominent Cherokees owned slaves, the Southern cause won the Cherokee Nation's official allegiance. When the war ended, the triumphant U.S. government had used a predictable means to punish the Civilized Tribes for their part in the rebellion. They forced the Tribes to cede portions of their western Territory lands to serve as homes for the Kiowa, Osage, Comanche, Arapaho, and others.

In the midst of the ceded portion, however, sprawled the "unassigned lands," or "Oklahoma," the "district" Pease had referred to. This section was held by no tribe, and for years land-hungry whites called Boomers had advocated the view that the district was not properly a part of the Indian Territory and should be opened for settlement.

Some of the most radical Boomers, led by a Kansan named David L. Payne, had attempted to establish settlements within the Indian Territory but had been driven out by Fort Reno troops assigned to protect the Territory. The Boomer movement now concentrated mostly on influencing Congress, and the conventional wisdom was that soon the Boomers would prevail in Washington.

Joe didn't doubt it. When government and Indian faced off, the Indian always lost. It was an old story for Joe. As a child, he had watched the white man maintain a political grip on the Indians of the Territory, even though those Indians were in theory supposed to be largely independent. Early on, cattlemen had trespassed on Territory grazing lands and had carved major cattle trails right through Indian lands to the Kansas cowtowns. To their credit, many cattlemen faithfully paid the per-head trail tolls charged by the tribes and enforced in the Cherokee Nation by the police organization called the Cherokee Light Horse. But many other cattlemen were defiant.

The worst part to young Joe had been seeing Indian men degrade themselves before white cattlemen, hoping for a handout. Even Sam Wolfkiller had done it from time to time, much to Joe's shame. It had always been heartbreaking to see Sam Wolfkiller grinning as he led away a scrawny longhorn already on its last legs, happy to have received a pittance from a Texas trail boss. Sam Wolfkiller had always said such placations were gifts. Joe had not agreed. Nothing bought at the price of a man's dignity was a gift in his book.

The railroad boom had changed the cattle business since those earlier cattle-drive days and changed the landscape in the process. Now smoking locomotives dragged long lines of freight and passenger cars across the Territory plains. Early in the previous decade, the Missouri, Kansas, and Texas Railroad had built a route southward through the heart of the Cherokee Nation, passing through Fort Gibson and providing a direct connection between Texas to the south and Kansas on the north. The Atchison, Topeka, and Santa Fe also ran a line through the enticing unassigned lands. There was talk that the tiny railroad stations along the Santa Fe would become instant cities once the government opened the district for settlement.

Pease rattled on about such changes until Joe was weary of it. As night fell and the riders prepared to make camp along an old cattle trail, Joe turned to Pease as the latter built a fire. "Why are you really riding with me?" he asked.

Pease seemed surprised. "I done told you. Because I want to make up for all them bad things before." He paused. "Don't you believe me, Joe?"

Joe didn't answer.

"There—see them?"

Pease was crouched alongside Joe Wolfkiller in a cluster of brush growing around the base of a cottonwood on the north bank of a little rivulet beside which they had stopped for water and rest. Far down a shallow grassland slope beyond them were two riders, slowly approaching.

"They saw us," Pease said.

"No," Joe replied. "I don't believe they did."

"They saw us," Pease reaffirmed. "I don't reckon it matters though."

"It can matter to me. I'm wanted here."

They were in the Cherokee Nation now, near the Neosho River and about twenty-five miles north of Fort Gibson. Since crossing the Territory border, Joe had been even more tense and distrustful of Pease then before. He had several reasons. For one thing, Pease was unwilling to discuss Sam Wolfkiller's purported illness at any length. Further, Pease had grown noticeably more nervous the farther they had gone. Nevertheless, Joe had continued riding with Pease, wondering if he were foolish for it.

"I'll go down and meet them, talk to them, just to keep everything friendly," Pease said abruptly.

"No!" said Joe.

It was too late. Pease was already standing and waving. He shouted a halloo and splashed across the rivulet. Joe swore and ducked lower in the brush.

Pease walked energetically down the slope toward the riders, who put their hands on their rifles as soon as they saw him. Pease reached them and talked with big gestures. The riders never unbooted their rifles. Finally Pease pointed back up the slope toward Joe.

When he started back up the slope again, the riders came with him.

Chapter 3

Joe Wolfkiller looked back at the dark eyes glittering at him from the other side of the campfire and thought the thoughts of a mouse surrounded by cats. The two riders Pease had greeted on the plain sat drinking coffee, talking to Pease about this and that, and casting discomforting glances at Joe. Their names, they said, were John Berg and Arasmus Little, and they were railroad men working for the Santa Fe line. Why they were out riding these parts alone they did not say.

Joe did not believe their story, nor did he even remotely trust Pease anymore. There was something unseen at work here, something hiding behind a facade of small talk and forced casualness. Joe determined that he would remain with Pease no longer, but he could not simply rise and leave, not with those two men watching him so closely. Berg's eyes reminded Joe of the pink orbs of the hog he had killed back in Hambone Coltrane's shed. Beyond that, there was something uncomfortably familiar about Berg.

Pease seemed different now that the others had joined them. He was jovial, almost giddy, cracking silly jokes and laughing at them, even when nobody else did. He walked around a lot, mouth running on, legs and arms in constant nervous motion. Joe chided himself for having ridden this far with him. True, Pease had introduced Joe to the newcomers by the false name of Henry Feather and said they were riding to seek jobs as deputies of Judge Parker over in Arkansas, but Joe did not feel the story was believed. The stares were too continual and suspicious.

19

"Mr. Feather, would you like a cup of coffee?" Berg asked.

"No. I don't drink coffee much."

"Smart Indian, smart Indian. The stuff keeps me from sleeping, but I can't bring myself to get shut of it. You're a sound sleeper, I'll bet, Mr. Feather."

"I sleep well."

"I'll bet you do, yes, sir." Berg stood and poured the remnants of his own coffee on the ground. "Well, I'm ready to turn in. Like as not, I'll lay awake two hours before I can get my eyes to stay shut. Then I'll have to wake up for a squirt. Too much coffee, that's what it is."

Joe felt his hackles rise. Berg's purposeless commentary was too artificial. Joe's hand, hidden beneath a blanket he had thrown over himself, slipped to the butt of his pistol.

But nothing happened. Berg spread his bedroll and crawled in, yawning broadly and snoring within five minutes despite his prediction of sleeplessness. The others spread their bedrolls as well.

Pease walked up to Joe and looked down at him questioningly. "Why you looking that way, Joe?" he whispered. "There ain't nothing wrong with them two."

Joe looked into Pease's eyes. "If I find you have lied to me, Pease, I'll see you repaid double for it."

Pease responded with only a vague grunt. "I'm turning in," he said, and headed for his bedroll.

It all came to a head exactly an hour and fourteen minutes later.

Joe Wolfkiller was huddled beneath his blankets, and though his body was weary, his mind was alive and racing. He had kept silent, feigning sleep, for more than an hour. He was still trying to fetch out the memory of whom Berg reminded him of, but mostly he was just waiting until he was sure the others were not awake, so he could make his run.

At last he decided to try. Making no noise, he sat up. The fire was a feeble flame on red embers, smoking up into the darkness. Snores rose from three bedrolls. Joe laid his blanket aside and began to stand. He was fully clothed, and his pistol was still holstered at his hip.

Berg rolled over and began to sit up just as Joe was on the verge of creeping toward the horses. Joe saw it, turned to the side, and pretended to beat something out of his blanket.

"What's wrong, Mr. Feather?" Berg asked softly.

"Spark from the fire," Joe replied. Inwardly he fumed. Now he would have to wait even longer.

"That right, Mr. Feather?" Berg asked—and right then Joe Wolfkiller knew him.

John Berg was a deputy of Judge Parker's court. Joe had seen him the very night Tom Pease had run out on him after the robbery that went sour. It made sense now. Pease had betrayed him. Probably his story of Sam Wolfkiller's illness was a lie designed to lure him across the Indian Territory border. No wonder Pease had been willing to help him buy a horse. For all Joe knew, Pease might have turned deputy himself.

The scene that followed was eerie and muted in the dim light of the fire and the dimmer light of the moon. Joe Wolfkiller tossed his blanket aside and rose, drawing his pistol at the same moment.

John Berg simultaneously threw his blanket aside to expose a sawed-off Greener shotgun to the red glow of the fire. "That's enough stirring around, right there, Cherokee Joe," Berg said. "You ain't going nowhere but to Arkansas."

At the same time, Little and Pease also came awake, if they had really been asleep at all, and threw aside their blankets to reveal drawn weapons. Pease had a pistol, Little a shotgun that was twin to Berg's.

"Well, Joe, looks like it's time for taking off masks, huh?" Pease said, laughing his giddy laugh.

"I'll kill you, Pease." Joe had not let go of his pistol.

"You're threatening a soon-to-be-reinstated deputy of the Arkansas court," Pease replied. "Bringing in Cherokee Joe ought to be enough to put me back in the judge's good graces."

"Drop that pistol, halfbreed," Berg ordered.

"That's right, Joe, drop it." Pease chortled. "Drop it and come in alive, and let Judge Parker see that the very deputy he fired for worthless is good enough to bring in Cherokee Joe."

Joe did not drop his pistol. "My father?" he asked Pease.

"Dead, Joe. Gunned down he was by Caul Slidell himself in a robbery down at the Guthrie rail station. He and a bunch of his redskin friends had hired out to freight something to the station for somebody or other. Picked a bad time to go—Slidell shot down three of them just for the fun of seeing a little Cherokee blood. Sam, he coughed up aplenty of it before he kicked off." Pease chortled.

"Drop the pistol, halfbreed," Berg commanded again.

Joe looked from face to face, all featureless in the fading red fireglow. He sighed loudly, then let his pistol fall to the ground.

Pease chuckled and stepped forward. Berg and Little lowered their shotguns and did the same, all eager to be the first to lay hand officially on the much-wanted Cherokee Joe, now a prisoner of Parker's court.

Joe Wolfkiller dropped with the speed of a stone. He landed flat on his stomach, sweeping up the pistol he had let fall. Little raised his shotgun and fired, but the shot passed a good two feet above Cherokee Joe's head. Joe's aim, not as hurried, was better. Little took the bullet in the stomach and buckled. Berg swore and fired off his Greener. Joe felt pellets fan past and plow the ground beside him. His responding shot passed through Berg's skull, killing him before he could fall.

Pease fired next, but he was scared and might as well have aimed at the sky. Joe rolled and fired three quick blasts that caught Pease in the chest so firmly that his feet kicked off the ground. He fell back, took one rattling breath, and died.

Little was still alive. Joe walked over to him and looked down. Little had lost his shotgun when he fell and now scrambled toward it. Joe kicked it away, then with a swing of the same foot kicked Little backward and down.

He raised his pistol and aimed it at Little's face. The deputy closed his eyes.

Joe diverted the pistol as he squeezed the trigger, sending the slug into the dirt beside Little's ear. He holstered the empty pistol, walked over to Little's shotgun, and picked it up. "If you live, you spread word," he said to Little, who was gasping for breath like a man pulled from a lake. "Tell it that Cherokee Joe is going to find Caul Slidell and kill him, and that he will take Slidell's scalp in return for the life of Sam Wolfkiller. You understand, Deputy?"

"Yes, yes." Little's voice sounded high-pitched with pain and fear. "Thank you, thank you for letting me live."

"Slidell—where can I find him?"

"Kansas, somewhere north of Great Bend. That's the best we've heard."

Joe turned and collected the guns from the fallen men, pausing long enough to spit in the face of Tom Pease as he reloaded his pistol. He considered taking Pease's scalp, but he had never scalped anyone before and was not sure how, so he didn't. There was another reason: He didn't want Little to see how badly he was shaking.

Joe Wolfkiller had always wondered what it would feel like to kill another man. Now he knew. It made him feel sick and scared.

The implications of what had happened were clear. This would mean the gallows for him if he was caught, and the thought scared him terribly, for he had a particular horror of hanging, having once witnessed such an execution during a visit with Sam Wolfkiller to Fort Smith.

Joe selected the best two horses from those hobbled nearby and saddled them with the best saddles. He would ride one as hard as he could, then switch to the other and ride hard some more. He took the saddlebags too, loaded with trail food and shells for the Greeners. Little still lay on the ground, moaning and watching Joe in silence. When Joe was done with his preparations, he mounted and rode off. He stopped shortly after he was out of sight of the camp, pausing only long enough to be sick. Then he rode on.

*   *   *

He rode as if the devil were nipping his tail. A murky moon sailed above, and cold air numbed his ears and nose. Hunger and thirst raged within, but he ignored them. He fancied he heard horsemen closing in upon him in the darkness, though he knew this was all but impossible. Not enough time had passed.

Joe rode for many hours before he stopped. Both mounts were dripping and exhausted by then, and Joe's head was reeling. He had grown too weary for the pretense of fearlessness that fooled most others and usually himself. He wished he had not told Little to spread word of his plans to kill Caul Slidell. Such talk would only make him seem all the more dangerous and murderous, and make capture and death on the gallows come all the sooner.

Joe hobbled the horses. He still felt sick in his stomach and tight in his groin, and every time he thought of his father's death, he suffered great waves of grief. Though Pease had proved untruthful, Joe did not doubt that he spoke truly about the shooting of Sam Wolfkiller, for Pease no longer had a motive to lie when he told him of that.

Joe wrapped himself in a blanket and lay down in a little ravine where he shivered and fought back the urge to weep. Soon it would be dawn. He desperately needed rest before continuing.

Dreams came with sleep. At first they were dreams of Parker's court, his jail, his gallows built to accommodate as many as a dozen doomed men. He dreamed of the somber face of George Maledon, Parker's efficient hangman. Joe had heard Maledon discussing his craft that day he had seen the hanging in Fort Smith. In his restless imaginings Joe now stood on the gallows, the twelve-by-twelve beam above his head, as Maledon slipped the noose over his head, placing its nine coils carefully in the empty place behind his left jawbone. He smelled the oily pitch Maledon coated his ropes with and heard Maledon's matter-of-fact voice in his ear: "Don't worry, Cherokee Joe, it'll be a quick passing for you. The secret of a clean hanging is an old prestretched rope and a good-size knot. You're a light fellow, so I'm dropping you eight feet and eight inches to make sure it's a good snap. You won't feel it, at least not much."

Then, shortly before they dropped the trap from under him, Joe twisted his head and saw Parker standing in his window, watching as he always watched the hangings he mandated.

Joe jerked awake. Maledon and the gallows vanished. Nothing now but the dark sky above and the wind through the grass. He fell asleep again, and again he dreamed.

But this time the dream was very different—and confusing, even in his sleep. He was no longer in the Indian Territory but in some mountainous green region, wearing the sparse clothing of a Cherokee hunter from long-past days. A rocky stream gushed down a lush hillside before him. A hazy, cloud-muted daylight permeated the scene. Joe felt a gnawing dread as his eyes were drawn to a deep pool in the midst of the stream. The pool began to move.

A great coiling glistening thing rose from the water, a horned and scaly beast with a body thick as the trunk of a large tree, ringed with brilliant colors that caught and amplified the light. The boulder-size head rose, reaching up nearly to the treetops, and then it looked at him, just as the sun pierced the clouds and struck it.

A lightning-bolt flash of reflected light emanated from a shining crystalline crest on the beast's forehead, struck Joe squarely in the face, and he fell back, covering his blinded eyes with his hands as the massive head came down upon him, the mouth open and dripping.

Joe yelled when he awoke and for a terrible moment thought his dream was not a dream, for a bright light still flashed in his eyes. He sat up and saw he was still in the ravine, damp with dew and shaking from cold and fear, and knew it had all been a vivid nightmare, for the light in his eyes was that of the rising sun.

He stood, relieved but still shaking, and wrapped his arms around himself. A shudder racked him from head to toe, and he took deep breaths until he was calm.

The horses grazed about fifty feet away, their legs still firmly hobbled. Joe had not taken the saddles off them. They lifted their heads and looked at him, standing side by side. And then Joe blinked in surprise, for he saw a third horse there.

He turned and saw a Cherokee man kneeling on a blanket not twenty feet from him. He was ancient and thin, wearing a pair of store-bought wool trousers, tall boots, and an oversized threadbare coat of faded blue, a coat like those the Union troops had worn more than two decades ago in the Civil War. The old man was staring deeply into his cupped hands and seemed as oblivious to Joe's presence as the morning sun.

Chapter 4

In the span of two breaths Joe Wolfkiller's pistol was leveled on the old man. "Who are you?" Joe demanded.

The old man drew his cupped hands closer to his face and frowned as if Joe's threatening voice were no more than an irritating distraction.

"I asked you who you are!" Joe said. The pistol was heavy and cold in his hand, and his muscles hurt from his tense sleep on hard earth in cold air. He was embarrassed to note that he was shaking.

The old man lowered his hands, sighed, and shook his head. He dug his left hand into a pocket of the coat, causing Joe a moment of uncertainty, but all he drew out was a little hide pouch. Whatever had been in his hands he enclosed carefully in the hide and thrust into his pocket. Only now did he look at Joe, a mildly exasperated expression on his face. "Hello, Joe Wolfkiller," he said. "I can tell you this much: There are riders coming from the southeast, and they will reach you soon if you do not run very fast and turn westward. If you had kept your mouth shut, I might have been able to tell you how many they are and how many guns they carry."

"Tell me who you are, or I will kill you," Joe said.

"I am the wind, the sun, the earth, the voice of the toad, and the eye of the eagle." After that grandiose pronouncement, the ancient man gave Joe a polite little tea-party smile like an old woman's, his black eyes crinkling until they almost vanished in the double handfuls of weathered wrinkles surrounding them.

"You are a fool, that I can see," Joe replied. He was wary of this strange old fellow. "What is your name?"

The silver-haired Indian shrugged. "What difference does a name make? But call me Bunyan if you wish. It is as good a name as any."

Joe thought that a peculiar name for an Indian. He lowered his pistol a little. "How do you know my name, Bunyan?"

"I know what the eagle knows. I fly across the earth and see all things. My skills as a magician have told me that before me stands the young man named Joe Wolfkiller, a great brave warrior feared and wanted by the white man."

Joe was beginning to wonder if this was real or just a continuation of his dreams. "What do you mean, a magician?"

The old man looked at the sky and shook his head again. His white hair was stiff as broom straw and all but rustled with each movement of his head. "How little do our young remember of the old ways!" he said, mostly to himself. "Now the young know only the ways of the white men and the white doctors, whose ways work well enough for their own but are often poison to the Cherokees." He looked squarely at Joe now. "I am a magician, a conjurer. I am wise in the old lore, and nothing escapes my knowledge."

"You know, then, that I'm thinking about killing you."

"Of course I know this, Joe Wolfkiller. But you would not be wise to slay me because I want to help you escape the great evil coming upon you."

"How can you help me, old babbler?"

The old fellow reached into his pocket again and with a broad grin pulled out the little pouch he had placed there earlier. "With this," he answered. "It tells me all I need to know. It is this crystal that told me your name and warned me of the danger coming."

"Crystal?" Now Joe understood. "A divining crystal?"

"The best divining crystal of them all."

"I don't believe in divining crystals. I believe in this." Joe shook the pistol.

"I had one of those too, and also believed in it very

much, but now I've got it no longer," the old man said. "I sold it to help me get money enough to buy that horse yonder and begin my journey."

"I have a journey of my own and no time to hear of yours, you old Raven Mocker." Joe holstered his pistol, now sure his unexpected companion was senile and harmless.

Until now, the old man's face had been lighted with a friendly expression. Now the lines of his face straightened and narrowed and he looked deeply offended. "I am no Raven Mocker," he said. "The Raven Mocker takes life—I seek to give it. I eat no man's heart. If you are wise, you will let me ride with you and listen to my counsel. Otherwise those who pursue you will kill you, Joe Wolfkiller. But first you must eat."

It was the food that finally led Joe Wolfkiller to accept the company of the old man who called himself Bunyan. From a large pocket stitched inside the oversized Union coat the old fellow pulled half a loaf of stale bread, some dried meat, and a small flour sack nearly filled with parched corn. Joe ate hungrily, feeling the food give him new strength. When it came time to ride again, Joe grumpily agreed to let the old man come along. "But if you get in my way, old babbler, or slow me down, I will leave you," Joe warned.

"We must ride straight west," the old man said.

"No. It's north for me, so I can reach the Territory border sooner."

"Very well, Joe Wolfkiller," the other replied. "North is the best direction for me, even if you should avoid it. But if you insist upon riding this direction, I must tell you that when we see the riders who are chasing you, I will be forced to leave you, for my quest is too important to be interrupted by death."

And so they rode north, the old man twenty paces behind Joe. Joe felt less panicked today than the day before. He did not push his horses as hard, feeling he had a good lead on any pursuers. Even so, he looked back repeatedly. All he saw was the slumped, almost comical figure of the old Cherokee astride his bone-bag horse. Joe wondered which was more thin and decrepit—horse or rider.

The sun rose higher and brightened the land, though a rising cloudbank scudding from the west raised the prospect of a murky midday and a rainy afternoon.

After a while the old Indian began a chanting refrain that he repeated endlessly: "*Ha wiye-hyuwe, Ha wiye-hyuwe, Ye we-yuwehe, Ha wiyehyu-uwe . . .*"

As the sky darkened at the end of the day, Joe felt fear rising again. Against that background the old man's song became irksome. At last he turned in his saddle. "Old babbler, close your mouth. You are as bothersome as a cricket in a corner."

"It is only the first lines of a song sung by mothers to babies," the old man replied. "Did not your mother sing the old songs to you, Joe?"

"My mother died giving me birth. And she was white. She would not have known the old songs."

"Ah, ah yes, I had forgotten that."

"You had not forgotten. You never knew. Crystal stones do not whisper words to old babblers, else they would have told our fathers long ago how to defeat the whites."

"If the crystal is powerless, then how, Joe Wolfkiller, did I know your name?" the old man asked.

Joe did not answer him. He was twisted in his saddle, looking at the southern horizon behind the older rider. The sun had met the cloudbank long before, but its rays still shone behind the clearer sky to the south, and in the glow Joe clearly saw a little line of riders approaching.

The old Indian also looked back. After gazing a few moments, he turned a wry look back to the halfbreed. "I told you," he said. "You should always listen when a wise conjurer speaks."

"Shut up," Joe said. "Ride down that way—there's a ravine. If we make the horses lie down in it and hide with them, they will go past us."

By the time Joe Wolfkiller and the old man crossed into Kansas, the halfbreed's attitude about the old man had changed. Of the three riders who had swept past the ravine, Joe had recognized two as deputies of Parker's court. He was surprised to have been pursued so closely so quickly. It could only have meant that the pursuing deputies had been close when he had the shoot-out with Pease and the others. Why there were so many deputies in that area Joe could only guess. Maybe they had hints that Caul Slidell or some other desperado was in the region.

Whatever the case, they had come far more quickly than Joe had expected, and the old self-proclaimed conjurer had been completely accurate in his prediction of the route by which pursuit would come. Joe wasn't ready to put his trust in divining crystals just yet, but he was impressed and interested in this Bunyan. Joe had come to believe that Bunyan wasn't his real name. It hardly sounded appropriate for a Cherokee conjurer, and from the way the old man smiled whenever the name called, Joe suspected that *Bunyan* was just a word the man had chosen because its ring was pleasant to his ear.

Crossing the Territory border had calmed Joe, though it hardly marked the end of his danger. He could be arrested in Kansas just as easily as in the Territory. Little, he figured, must have lived, at least long enough to find the other deputies and tell them the direction his assailant had fled. Joe told himself that he hoped Little was as dead as the others now, but he knew it wasn't true. The killing of Pease and Berg still left a bad taste in Joe's mouth, though he would never have admitted it to anyone else.

It shouldn't be that way. Vengeance and the appreciation of battle was an ancient part of the Cherokee tradition that Joe saw as his heritage. Yet every time he thought about the gun battle, he felt as if snakes were swimming in his stomach.

Supper was more dried meat and parched corn. They built no fire.

"Tell me more about your quest," Joe asked his companion. "Where are you bound?"

"I'm bound for Hays City," the old man said. His voice was creamy with age, worn smooth as a century-old doorstep. "There I will find the one I seek—or so my crystal tells me."

"Where did you get your crystal?"

"From my father, who died on the Trail of Tears and was a greater conjurer even than me until he became a Baptist preacher and had to give it up. The crystal came to him from my grandfather, and it had come to my grandfather from his mother's brother, back in the days of his youth when he lived in the town of Kanuga in the land that used to be our people's. Where it came from before that I will not tell, for it is a great secret."

"Is who you are going to find a secret too?"

"No secret. I am going to find my daughter and give to her a great treasure." He smiled the old-lady smile again and glanced around slyly.

"A treasure? What kind of treasure?"

"I will speak no more of it," he said.

"Tell me, Bunyan. I want to know what this treasure is."

The old man still refused to talk. Joe pressed a new question. "Why is your daughter in Hays City?" he asked.

"I will sleep now," the old man said abruptly. He spread his blankets, lay down, and quickly began snoring.

He truly is crazy, Joe thought as he watched the old man sleep. As crazy as a mad dog. But his talk of treasure may not be crazy. Maybe it is a treasure he will be willing to share... or perhaps he will find himself sharing it whether he wills it or not.

Such thoughts made Joe feel strong and dangerous, and he enjoyed them as he drifted off to sleep.

When Joe woke up, the old man was sitting alone in the dawn light looking into his hands again, but this time he wasn't consulting his divining stone. He was reading from a book covered with a homemade binder of fringed leather. When he looked up and saw Joe blearily watching him, the old man smiled. "A quest is a wonderful thing," he said. "I have told you of mine. What is yours, that put the riders onto your trail?"

He doesn't know about the killings, Joe thought. *Divining stone or not, he doesn't know.*

"My quest is to go north of Great Bend, find a man named Caul Slidell, and kill him," Joe replied.

"I have heard of this Slidell," the old man said. "He is a bad white man. Is that why you wish to kill him?"

"He killed my father, Sam Wolfkiller, at the railroad station in Guthrie."

"Yes. I heard that Sam Wolfkiller was dead, but I did not know it was Caul Slidell who killed him."

"You knew my father?"

"I know all men. Most of them, at least."

They rode, side by side this time. "You still have not told me why you were chased by these riders that my crystal foresaw," the old man said.

"I had trouble in the Territory. I was forced to flee."

"Did this trouble involve killing?"

"Why should I tell you? Tell me about this treasure instead."

"It is a treasure for my daughter alone. When she has it, I can be at peace."

"If you won't talk about the treasure, talk about your daughter. Is she pretty?"

The old man's answer was less ready this time. "She was pretty when last I saw her. She was pretty like a tiny flower held in my arms."

Joe took a moment to understand. "You haven't seen her since she was a baby?"

"No."

"Who raised her?"

"A family that is now in Hays City."

"A white family?"

A pause. "There was no other way. My wife died giving her birth, just like your mother did. I could not care for her well enough alone. The white man and his wife, they said they would raise her like she was their child, and I gave her up to them."

"Your crystal could find no better way, eh?"

"Don't scoff at powerful things, Joe Wolfkiller. The crystal told me your name. It told me of your danger, and of the riders' coming. It saved your life."

"Then why couldn't it tell you what trouble I was in?" The awe that Joe had experienced after seeing the riders pass as predicted was falling away as his usual cynical skepticism regained ground.

"I told you: Do not scoff at the crystal. It is a dangerous thing to do."

Joe looked darkly at the old man. "Are you threatening me, old babbler?"

"It is no threat to give a warning to one who is in danger."

"Am I in danger, old man?"

"Cherokee Joe, they say, is always in danger. And any near him, they are in danger too."

"Then why are you riding with me?"

"Because our paths lie over the same ground. Besides, I like you. Me and my crystal, maybe we can keep you alive."

"So I can grow old and silver-haired and babble like you? That doesn't sound good to me. Once Caul Slidell is dead, I don't care what happens to me. I ride a death road, old man."

"Then you do need me," the other said. "I have been riding that same road for many days now."

"What does that mean?"

"My crystal. It has told me that soon I am going to die."

Chapter 5

When they entered the southeastern corner of Sedgwick County, the old Indian pulled his scrawny horse to a halt, took a deep breath, slid out of the saddle, and collapsed on the ground.

Joe, riding slightly in the lead again, was a hundred yards ahead before he heard the man's feeble cry for help. Joe reined in, turned, and saw him rolling from side to side on the ground, moaning and gripping his middle. By the time Joe galloped back to him, he had emptied the meager contents of his stomach onto the ground beside him.

Joe leaped down from his saddle and ran to his side. "Old babbler, what's wrong with you?" he said, kneeling.

"I am dying," the old man moaned.

"Dying? You can't die here."

"It seems as good a place to die as any."

Joe had no idea what to do. "Come on, you white-headed fool. Get up and get on your ugly horse."

"No, no. I can't." He hacked and spat up a little more, making a sour face afterward. "Joe Wolfkiller, can you read?" he asked.

"Yes, some."

"Good. In my saddle pouch, the old book..."

Joe rose, disturbed by all this and wishing he had never taken up with the old man. He opened the saddle-bag and found it stuffed with bottles and bags of unidentifiable concoctions, assorted clay and corncob pipes, and tobacco in a tin. The leather-covered book was in the midst of it all. He retrieved it and went to the old man's side.

"Read to me as I die."

"Which part?"

"Just open it and read."

Joe opened the book and squinted at the title page. The book was *Pilgrim's Progress*, written by someone named John Bunyan. Joe immediately knew from where the old man had borrowed his name.

Joe thought back to his days in the Indian Agency school. "Isn't this a book of the white man's religion?" he asked.

"Yes. A grand book, the story of a quest."

"What use does a Cherokee conjurer have with such a book?"

"I am not only a Cherokee conjurer," the old man said. "I am also a Methodist."

"I didn't think a good Methodist was supposed to be a conjurer too."

"I said I was a Methodist. I did not say I was a good one." The old man writhed and gripped his stomach more tightly. "Read, Joe. Read before I die!"

Joe flipped open the book, picked a place at random, and began to read. He was a poor reader and stumbled through the old-fashioned text in a jerky monotone. "'About the midst of this valley I perceived the mouth of hell to be, and it stood also hard by the wayside. Now, thought Christian, what shall I do? And ever and anon the flame and smoke would come out in such abundance, with sparks and hideous noises. . . .'"

"No, no. Do not read the fearsome parts," the old man directed. "Go to the end. Read of the end of the quest at the Celestial City."

Joe flipped farther, to the final pages. He found many of the words difficult to decipher. Sometimes the old man would give him the right ones from memory. "'Now I saw in my dream that these two men went in at the gate: and lo, as they entered, they were transfigured and they had raiment put on that shone like gold. There was also one that met them with harps and crowns, and gave them to them—the harps to praise withal, and the crowns in token of honor. Then I heard in my dream that all the bells in the city rang again for joy, and that it was said unto them, "Enter yet into the joy of your Lord." I also heard the men themselves, that they sang with a loud voice, saying, "Blessing, honor, glory, and power be to him that sitteth upon the throne, and to the Lamb, for ever and ever.'"

"Yes, that is the part," the old man said, relaxing now and smiling with his eyes closed. "Read more to me, Joe Wolfkiller."

Joe read for several more minutes with wearying difficulty. "'And after that, they shut up the gates, which when I had seen, I wished myself among them.'"

Joe paused and glanced down at the old man. His eyes were closed, and he was breathing deeply, asleep with a look of calm and peace on his face. Joe closed the book, laid it on the ground, then gathered wood and built a fire to keep the old man warm. It was foolish and dangerous for Joe to stay long in one place, so he thought about remounting his horse and leaving his companion alone. But thinking about it was as far as it went.

Two hours later, near dusk, the old man opened his eyes and sat up. Joe was crouched nearby by the fire, roasting a rabbit he had snared.

"Am I alive?" the Cherokee asked, looking around. "This does not look like the Celestial City."

"Ask your divining crystal, Will Ax," Joe said sharply.

The old man blinked. "How did you learn my name?"

"From your book. It told me a lot more than your old stone ever could. I picked it up again while you slept. Your name was written inside the cover." Joe glared at his companion. "I've called you a fool, but it's me who was the biggest fool, taking up with a man everyone in the Cherokee Nation knows is insane. My father told me about you long ago, Will Ax. He said you were crazy and that no one with sense came near you. He said you called yourself a conjurer but really were nothing but a fool whose chants could not even quiet a sleepless baby. I remember how he ran you away from our house one time when you came to steal. I should have recognized you."

Will Ax looked sheepish. "Your father sometimes spoke

words too harsh," he said. "I did not come to steal that day. I came to borrow."

"With you there is no difference. You have never repaid anything you owe. That's another thing everyone knows." Joe chuckled mirthlessly. "When you told me my name without being told it, I thought that maybe you really were a magician. Now I know that you knew me because you had seen me before."

"I admit that I knew you . . . but the crystal reminded me of your name."

"I do not believe in your crystal, babbler. Tell me— the men who chased me . . . you had seen them coming?"

Will Ax sighed and seemed to wither even more. "Very well, Joe. I admit that I saw them. I warned you for your father's sake. I knew you were the son of Sam Wolfkiller, who I have always thought of as my friend, even if he did not think of me as his."

"And I thank you for the warning. But I don't thank you for lying to me and keeping your real name from me, or for trying to make me believe you are something you aren't."

Will Ax's eyes were like those of a beaten pup. He rubbed his stomach gingerly.

"I still feel the death within me," he said.

"What you feel is the air in your gut, or the worms that keep you so scrawny," Joe returned. "I have wasted enough time with you, Will Ax. Starting tomorrow, I ride alone."

Will Ax made a pitiful and lonely sight the next morning when Joe Wolfkiller rode out. The old Cherokee, who had moaned and tossed all night, stood looking wistfully after Joe as he rode away. Joe topped a rise and glanced back at the camp, and suffered a pang of doubt. Maybe Will Ax really was sick. As angry as Joe still felt and as inconvenient, cumbersome, and dangerous a piece of baggage as Will Ax was, Joe didn't feel quite right about abandoning an old man in bad circumstances.

He rode over the rise, out of Will Ax's sight, and stopped to weigh the situation. Like Will Ax, he had a quest to fulfill. Somewhere to the northwest beyond the town of Great Bend he expected to find Caul Slidell, murderer of his father. The blood of Sam Wolfkiller cried out for vengeance. There was no place or time in Joe's life right now for a sick old man who would only be in the way. Joe spurred his horse and went on.

An hour later, he was glad of his decision. With Will Ax far behind, he felt free and purposeful. Let Will Ax deal with his own problems and fulfill his own quest. Likely as not, the whole thing—daughter, treasure, and all—was just some delusion anyway. If Will Ax had a treasure on him, Joe certainly hadn't seen it. Probably the old man's notion of treasure was his old book and that useless divining crystal.

Joe had known many older Cherokee men who were much like Will Ax, clinging to old notions but freely mixing in the white man's beliefs. Sam Wolfkiller had been a little like that, living in two worlds at the same time, fluctuating between them as Will Ax fluctuated between his self-styled Cherokee mysticism and the Christianity allegorized in his leather-bound Bunyan volume. Even Joe was somewhat the same way, though he usually didn't recognize it. Consciously he regarded the white half of his heritage with contempt, but there were times when a contradictory attitude buried deeper in his mind crept through, and he found himself despising his swarthy skin, his dark eyes, his shining black hair, his high cheekbones. He was embarrassed sometimes at the traditions and superstitions of his people and had refused to learn the old formulas and legends that men like Will Ax put such stock in. Only one part of his Indian heritage did he hold to dearly, though in a personalized and distorted form—the law of revenge.

The Cherokees and other Indians of old, his father had explained to him, had lived by a clear-cut code of revenge, a law of blood. This was no anarchistic, unbridled vengeance but a controlled, governed system of retribution, following strict guidelines of tribe, clan, kinship. It regulated Cherokee society and interaction in much the same way the white men's laws, courts, jails, and gallows regulated theirs. As time passed and the white men's ways had taken over, the Cherokees substantially abandoned their law of blood. Perhaps, Sam Wolfkiller had said, that was for the best. Perhaps the old system could no longer work in a world far less simple than it once had been.

As Joe had grown, he had often thought about the old law of blood, and as his life had become more troubled, had redefined that law to himself in his own simplified fashion. Joe's law was this: Any who strike me and my kin will be struck in turn, no matter what the cost. Violence for violence, blood for blood. There was no sophistication to the law of blood as Joe had rewritten it. It was simple, direct, uncompromising, and most of all, personal.

That was why Caul Slidell had to die, no matter what effort it took.

Joe rode until the darkness was thick, then made camp. His horse grazed the brown winter-dried grass. Joe dug out a handful of Will Ax's parched corn and ate, then lay down to sleep, his stomach still grumbling. He had taken only a little food from his former companion; soon he would have to find more.

When Joe awakened the next morning, Will Ax was with him again, sitting looking at his divining crystal as he had the first morning. Joe sat up and swore.

Will Ax looked at him, grinned, and put away his crystal. "I have bread," he said. "Good bread, baked by a white woman. A wagon came by after you left our camp, carrying a family toward the Territory border. I put on a mean face and asked food from them. They gave it to me very fast because they were afraid of me; the children begged me not to take their scalps. When I had the bread, I thought my friend Joe might want some too, so I came to bring you some."

Joe, still seated, drew his knees up and put his head between them. Will Ax, it seemed, was like a shadow. He could not get rid of him. At least he had brought good food. Joe accepted half a loaf of bread and ate hungrily.

Will Ax ate more slowly, seated on his haunches; then stood, grasped his stomach again, and fell to one side. "I think, Joe, that you need to take me to Wichita."

"Why? You wish to die there?"

"No. My crystal told me I would not die . . . but only if I will see a white doctor."

"Your crystal is as crazy as you are, old man."

*   *   *

The doctor's name was Lansford, and he had taken it in his head a month before that he had missed his calling and should have been a novelist instead of a physician. Lately he had begun closing his office two days a week to devote himself to his first epic, *Bernard DuBrendle: Army Scout and Slayer of Savages*, subtitled *A Narrative of a Hero of the American Western Plains*. He was in the midst of a particularly bloody passage in which his hero was wiping out yet another dozen heathens with remarkably simple minds and easily crushed skulls.

He was preparing to face DuBrendle off with the most savage and heathen of them all, Scalpyanker, the narrative's brutal villain of unspecified tribe and background, when a knock on his door interrupted him. Swearing beneath his breath at illiterate fools who can't read posted hours on a closed door, he shouted, "I'm closed! Come back tomorrow!"

Another vigorous knock threatened to rattle the door off its hinges. This time Lansford did not bother to keep his oath beneath his breath. He tossed his script-covered pad on the desktop, rose, and stomped to the door.

His plan was to pull open the door and give a vigorous lecture to whoever was on the other side, but when the door opened, his plan immediately changed. Looking back at him was a living personification of his fictional Scalpyanker, a lean but muscled fire-eyed Indian with shocks of long black hair spilling out from under both sides of his hat. Dr. Lansford drew in his breath and felt faint.

"Open the door," Scalpyanker said softly but authoritatively.

Dr. Lansford, beginning to tremble, obeyed. The Indian led in another, this one old and frail, his face as innocuous and pleasant as the first's was fierce and frightening.

"Listen, I'm not open for business today." Lansford cleared his throat. "Besides that, I don't treat..."

"Yes, you do treat Indians, starting today," Joe Wolfkiller said. "And you are open for business."

Dr. Lansford swallowed. "Yes. It seems I am." His eyes flickered to Will Ax. "Him or you?"

"Him."

"All right. You can wait outside."

"I'll wait here."

"Of course. Of course."

Lansford had Will Ax sit in a straightback chair. "And just who are you, old fellow?" he asked.

"I am the wind, the sun, the earth, the voice of the toad, and the eye of the eagle," Will Ax said.

"Never mind who he is," Joe said. "Just fix him."

"What's wrong with you?" Lansford asked Will Ax.

"There is a sharp stick inside of me, or perhaps a gnawing bug is eating my entrails."

"He means his stomach is bad," Joe said.

"I see."

"The old formulas have failed to drive out the affliction."

"'Old formulas'? Old heathen superstitions, you mean. You people are your own worst enemies, the nonsense you go by. Take off that coat and shirt so I can feel your belly."

Joe took the coat and hung it on a wall peg behind a partition on the other side of the office. The doctor, growing more used to his unusual visitors, probed and poked Will Ax, examined his tongue and eyes, and asked questions. Finally he pulled the partition over and behind it conducted a closer examination.

At last he came back around it to Joe. "He's full of worms, head to toe," he said. "Worst case I've seen, but no more than I'd expect in an—" His discretion stopped him just in time. "Anyway, I've got something over here that ought to scour them right out of him. You might want to take some yourself. If you've been much around him, you've probably got them too."

The doctor went to his shelf and selected a dark bottle. He poured some of its contents into a smaller bottle and corked it. Handing it to Joe, he gave directions for its use.

"How much money?" Joe asked.

The doctor, wanting only to have the Indians out of his office, waved his hand. "Free. Take it. Another gift from the white man to the red."

The comment was not well taken. "I can pay as well as any white man. I don't want gifts," Joe said coldly.

The doctor knew he had blundered and quickly named a price. Joe thrust his hand into his pocket to get the meager wad of money remaining.

It was gone.

Joe was stunned. He couldn't guess what had happened to the money. More than likely, he had simply dropped it sometime during his ordeals and flights.

The doctor stood looking at him with barely concealed contempt; obviously he figured Joe was about to tell him he had nothing and take the medicine for nothing after all. "You have no money?" the doctor ventured.

"No, but I can pay." Joe turned and walked over to Will Ax's coat on the wall. Will Ax was still behind the partition, slowly putting his smelly clothing back on. Joe reached into the pocket of Will's coat and withdrew the hide bundle containing the divining crystal.

"Here," he said, handing it to the doctor.

"What is it?"

Joe whispered, not wanting Will Ax to hear. "It is a Cherokee divining crystal. Very valuable."

Dr. Lansford took the bundle, opened it, and peered at the crystal. This was the first time Joe had seen it—a bullet-shaped clear stone with a red streak up the middle. It was a beautiful quartzlike object, not quite like anything Joe had seen.

"It's remarkable," Lansford said, holding it up. "Absolutely remarkable. I'll consider it fair payment."

He pocketed the stone as Will Ax came around the partition. "I think I won't die now, Joe," Will said.

"Good for you," Joe mumbled.

"Don't let anyone see you leaving," Lansford said. "I don't want it out that I've taken to treating Indians."

Chapter 6

Joe Wolfkiller slept little that night, not solely because of the violent storm that rolled in as the sun set or the hardness of the packed floor of the woodshed in which he and Will Ax had taken shelter. It was primarily dreams that kept Joe restless.

He and the old man were just north of Wichita, still in sight of the town. Joe would have liked to go farther, but Will Ax remained sick all day and could not travel well. The horses had also seemed weary and hungry, so north of town Joe had set up dry camp in a well-hidden dry gully, sneaked to the nearest barn and stolen grain for the horses, and sat stewing in dissatisfaction, smoking one of Will Ax's pipes to pass the time as the old man took his rest and medicine.

By evening, the storm was beginning to well up, and Joe put them on the move again, looking for night shelter. Near a three-story clapboard house with gables and four chimneys they had found this substantial woodshed and moved in, Joe figuring that whoever was in the house would certainly be unlikely to come poking around in the shed during a storm. He tethered the horses at a streamside grove nearby, out of sight of the house.

Will Ax, who seemed to be feeling much better, had begun talking as soon as they settled down in the woodshed, his voice a steady low monotone. The old man had been somber all evening, talking about his long-lost daughter and hoping he would be able to find her before he died.

44

"How do you know you will die?" Joe asked. "That crystal is just a piece of rock." He at once regretted having mentioned the divining stone, for Will Ax did not yet know it had gone as payment for his medicine. Joe was not eager for the moment Will discovered he no longer had the stone.

"The crystal is not an ordinary stone. It's like no other crystal still in this world, and there will be no others like it to come."

"Maybe so. But it would take more than a piece of stone to make me believe I was going to die."

"The crystal is never wrong," Will Ax said. After a few moments, though, he added, "Well, that is not really true, not anymore. In the old days the crystal always spoke truly. Now sometimes it doesn't speak at all—" Will Ax leaned forward and whispered, "and sometimes it speaks lies. I think it is like me. It is getting old and hard to get along with."

They slept, and Joe's dreams started afresh. At first he relived the shooting of the deputies down in the Cherokee Nation, and dreamed of flight and pursuit, but this gave way to the same bizarre dream that had awakened Joe that first morning Will Ax joined him. Once again Joe saw himself garbed as an ancient Cherokee, standing beside the same deep mountain pool. The dark water stirred, and from its surface emerged the great serpentine head with horns and a crescent-shaped light that shone from its forehead, a light glancing off of, perhaps out of, a crystalline stone that was mystifyingly familiar. The light flashed into Joe's eyes, blinding him. Great fear overwhelmed him. He tossed and rolled and tried to wake up, for in the dream his legs would not move even though the Uktena was coming at him to kill him. . . .

Uktena. Even as Joe awoke, he realized what the dream beast was. Memory raced back to childhood and dark nights in the cabin near Tahlequah. He recalled sitting at the feet of Sam Wolfkiller and hearing stories of the former days of his people. Several of those stories had dealt with the great Uktena, a serpentine water dragon that haunted the dark pools and gaps of the eastern mountains along the bounds of the Cherokee ancient world. The Uktena, beautiful yet terrible to behold, was the most dangerous of the monster beasts of Cherokee folklore, for to see it was enough to bring suffering and tragedy, and the stench of its breath carried death.

Joe sat up. The storm was raging outside, wind-driven rain pounding the shed roof and sprinkling in through the gaps and knotholes of the walls. As Joe peered out the largest hole, a brilliant lightning flash struck him in the eyes. He remembered how upon awakening from the dream that first time, he had been looking into the sun. This time it must have been the lightning that accounted for the light from the Uktena's brow... but why had he twice dreamed of a legendary beast he had not thought of since childhood?

Joe turned and was surprised to see a figure standing in the darkness facing him. Half a moment later he knew it was only Will Ax, but during the brief span of confusion and lingering fear from the nightmare, the old Cherokee's presence was startling. More lightning flashed and illuminated the weathered old face. Joe was surprised to see water trailing from Will's eyes.

Will Ax's voice was slightly broken when he spoke. "You shouted just now," he said. "You shouted of an Uktena."

"I dreamed of one," Joe said. "How loud did I shout?"

Will Ax ignored Joe's question and asked his own. "Do you know why you have dreamed of the Uktena?"

"No, no. Listen to me—did I shout so loud, someone could have heard me from the house?"

"I can tell you why," Will Ax aid. "It is because you have been in the presence of the *ulunsuti* stone."

"What are you talking about, old man?"

"My divining crystal." Will Ax paused. Another lightning flash ripped the sky; the wind that came through the knotholes was cold. "I will tell you my secret now—why the divining crystal is so great a thing. It is not just a crystal like most of the magicians have. It is an *ulunsuti*, the last *ulunsuti* there ever will be, taken many years ago from the brow of the last Uktena."

Joe remembered more of the lore he had heard at his

father's knee long ago—how the stone on the brow of the Uktena, the *ulunsuti* stone, was the greatest divining crystal any Cherokee seer could hope to possess. From it he could learn of things past, present, and future. He could predict the outcome of illness, good or bad. With it he could make rain, win the love of women, become a great hunter, and foretell the fate of warriors going to battle.

"But there cannot really be an *ulunsuti* stone," Joe said. "Such things are nothing but old stories. Uktenas, *ulunsutis*—they are lies."

Will Ax sat down wearily. "It does not matter now, I guess. The *ulunsuti* is gone anyway."

Joe's stomach knotted. "I know," he confessed. "I gave your crystal to the doctor to pay for the medicine."

Will Ax took the news quietly. "Forgive my tears, unfitting for a man," he said after a while. "I can't help but cry. The *ulunsuti* was the treasure I was carrying to my daughter. Now I have nothing to give her at all." He sighed. "Perhaps it was no longer a treasure anyway. I've not kept the *ulunsuti* the way it should be kept, and I believe that's what made it sick. It doesn't do what it is supposed to. White men, they are supposed to die when they see the *ulunsuti*. But the white doctor—he did not die when you gave it to him?"

"He did not die."

"I thought so. The *ulunsuti*'s strength is fading. It is old and sick and ready to die, like me."

At that moment the shed door burst open. In the doorway stood a man in a hat, longjohns, and a slicker. He held a shotgun with one arm; a lighted lantern swung from the other. He looked the surprised pair over. "Up nice and slow, you trespassing redskins," he said. "I thought I heard somebody squall out here. Now, which ort I to do—shoot you down, or take you in to see Mr. Christmas?"

Will Ax lifted his hands above his head, shrugged, and said, "If it's up to us to choose, I think maybe we'd rather go meet Mr. Christmas."

After disarming his prisoners, the man hustled them through the rain into a back door of the house and immediately to the left into a small windowless room. He closed the door and locked it from the outside. Joe fumbled in the darkness until he found a lamp with a box of matches beside it. He lighted the lamp. Will Ax's face was gaunt with fright.

The wall was papered with old newspapers and covered with framed pictures, documents, and the like. The only furniture in the room was a desk, lamp table, and three chairs. Will Ax sat down, but Joe paced about the room like a caged cougar. Neither man spoke. Both knew that bad luck had just come their way.

Time passed, and no one came to the room. Joe kept pacing and finally began studying the pictures and documents on the wall. He had the impression this was some sort of makeshift and generally unused office. At length he came to one framed portrait hanging near a corner and stopped in his tracks.

Looking back at him was the photographed face of Judge Isaac Parker. Scrawled across the base of the picture were the words *To my good friend and supporter, James R. Christmas. Isaac Parker, United States Judge, Western District of Arkansas, 1886. Best wishes to you, Jim.*

Joe Wolfkiller swore aloud.

The door rattled and opened. In walked the man who had caught them in the woodshed. He still had his shotgun. With him was another man, very tall and slender with bushy red hair and wiry sideburns that met the ends of a broad orange mustache.

"There they be, Mr. Christmas."

The red-haired man strode in and examined the prisoners as if they were statues on display in a gallery. He looked at Joe Wolfkiller a long time, then walked over to the desk, opened it, and removed a wooden box from which he took a long cigar. He made a slow and deliberate show of biting off the end and lighting up, his wide-spaced eyes on Joe all the time.

When the cigar was burning to his satisfaction, he exhaled a thick cloud and sat on the corner of the desk. "Mr. Miller," he said to the armed man, "do you realize that you have just captured Cherokee Joe?"

Miller's eyes bugged. "No! You don't mean it!"

"Indeed I do. Judge Parker only today wired me that Cherokee Joe was thought to be heading into Kansas. Seems he gunned down some deputies in the Cherokee Nation. He asked me to keep my eyes and ears open. I wager he'd be surprised to find that the subject himself has shown up, literally on my doorstep."

Joe felt a cold dread that left him struggling not to tremble. He let nothing show on his swarthy face.

Christmas smiled coldly at Joe. "You've gone one up on your own reputation in the last little stretch, Cherokee Joe. You've suddenly become quite a talked-about villain in these parts."

Joe stared back at him, saying nothing.

"Perhaps you're surprised that I'm so well informed about such recent events in the Indian Territory," Christmas said to Joe, puffing his cigar languidly. "The reason is simple. I and Judge Parker—you know the famed 'Hanging Judge,' I'm sure—enjoy a longtime association. I've helped him out several times in locating Indian Territory criminals who've fled this way, and he has shown his appreciation by regularly sending me wires, fliers, and the like concerning those he suspects might come over the border. Several months ago he sent me a sketch of 'Cherokee Joe' Wolfkiller, even before your most recent violent exploit. It's a good likeness." Christmas turned to Will Ax. "But this old fellow, I confess, I don't recognize."

Joe expected Will Ax to launch into his usual self-identification with wind, sun, earth, and so on, but this time Will answered in a lifeless tone, "My name is Will Ax." Joe noted how different Will Ax was, no spark in his eye, no joviality. It's because of the *ulunsuti*, Joe thought. It's gone, and it took his spirit with it.

Will Ax gave Joe a tired but searching look. Tonight was the first time the old man had heard the nature of the crime that had Joe on the run. Joe wondered if the knowledge would alter Will's apparent affection for him.

"Will Ax!" Christmas declared. "I've heard of you, after all, old fellow. Crazed Cherokee eccentric from the Territory. And crazed you must be to ride with the likes of this murderous young heathen." He waved his cigar toward Joe.

"Let him go," Joe said. "He has done nothing."

"Well, I wouldn't say that. He's trespassed on my property, far outside the reserved Cherokee grounds. And he's fraternizing with a known killer."

Will Ax, still seated, looked like a dried-up sad old sack of bones. He raised no protest at his detention or any plea for release.

Christmas spoke to Miller. "Take the old one out. Lock him upstairs. I want to talk to Cherokee Joe alone."

Miller obeyed. Joe stood where he was, looking contemptuously at Christmas.

"Don't think of attempting to escape," Christmas said, taking a small pistol from his pocket. "I'll not hesitate to use this if you try anything."

"You intend to turn me over to Parker?"

"Not necessarily. There's something you can do for me. You can earn your freedom—if you will cooperate."

Joe had not expected to hear anything like this. "What do you mean, 'cooperate'?"

Christmas smiled. "Cherokee Joe, your arrival here is fortuitous—for both of us, whether you can believe that or not. I have a strong suspicion that I know what you're up to. I heard about Caul Slidell's murder of your father. Knowing the attitude you are reported to have about such things, I suspect you are on your way to get your revenge on Caul Slidell for gunning down your father."

"And if I am?"

"Well, then, Joe, if you are, you and I are in a position to strike a deal that will let you avenge yourself against Slidell and let me do a great favor for my good friend Judge Parker."

Joe's expression remained the same, but in his narrow eyes Christmas saw a spark of cautious interest.

"If there is a man Judge Parker is eager to see captured at the moment, it's Slidell. Parker wants him even more than he wants you. Slidell and his hellriders have been a thorn in the side of the Arkansas court too long. I'm in the position of owing Judge Parker a few favors, and I'd like to even the balance by being the man to deliver Caul Slidell to his doorstep."

"What does that have to do with me?"

"Simple. I want you to go out and capture Slidell for me. Bring him back here. I have plenty of capable men in my hire who can ensure that Slidell is delivered the rest of the way back to Judge Parker's jail."

"Then why don't you send these 'capable men' to get Slidell? Why send me?"

"Because it's one thing to deliver a trussed-up prisoner from Kansas to Fort Smith. It's another thing to capture him in the first place. That requires a cunning, a skill, a ruthlessness—and especially a motivation—that my men don't possess. You, though—you're a different story altogether. I know enough about you to feel sure that you can do the job. And you already want to get him."

"I don't want to bring Slidell back alive. I want to kill him."

"Oh, but that won't do at all, Joe. You bring Slidell back to me alive, or else."

"Or else what?"

"Else your friend Will Ax never leaves this house alive. You see, Cherokee Joe? That's the special motivation you'll have. Caul Slidell, delivered safe to my hands, or your friend as dead as last January."

Christmas puffed his cigar again and smiled.

Chapter 7

Joe Wolfkiller rode through the cold Kansas air on a fine black mount provided by Christmas. His guns, too—a Winchester saddle rifle and a Colt Peacemaker—were of highest quality and out of Christmas's private arms stock.

Joe had accepted Christmas's bargain because he saw no other option save sacrificing Will Ax's life. He suspected there was far more to this bizarre setup than he had been told. Christmas's story didn't ring true. Why would a man who was an associate and supporter of the staunchest law-and-order judge in the American territories set up such an illegal machinery as this just to bring in a criminal as a friendly favor for the court? Christmas was taking a risk by holding Will Ax hostage. Indians had few enough rights, but even they could not be kidnapped and held hostage under threat of death.

Joe's curiosity was high about the whole business. Overwhelming even that curiosity, however, was a rising feeling of desperation. It had been one thing to set off to kill Caul Slidell, which could be done from a distance with a bullet. It was a far different thing to be charged with bringing Slidell in alive within five weeks, the deadline set by Jim Christmas. How could he hope to do it?

Joe's route out of the Wichita area roughly followed the Arkansas River and the route of the Missouri Pacific Railroad that extended down from its junction with the Rock Island and Santa Fe lines at the town of Hutchinson. Joe's horse was a fast traveler and served him well, and by nightfall he was near the common line dividing Sedgwick and Reno counties.

He slept later than he had planned the following morning, for the journey had tired him, and his black slipped its hobbles and wandered off, requiring him to hunt it down. He set off as quickly as he found it but already had lost three hours. Crossing the county line, he continued along the Arkansas River toward Hutchinson.

It was nearly dusk when he spotted a wagon parked by the roadside. Even in the waning light, this wagon was hard to miss. It had paneled sides and a high seat and somewhat resembled a circus wagon except for its plain white paint and slightly smaller size. On the panels were black letters that became legible as Joe drew closer: *PATRICK ST. PATRICK—QUALITY PORTRAITS MADE CHEAP*.

Joe was initially wary of the wagon, for even chance encounters with strangers had to be considered dangerous in his circumstances. He figured to pass the wagon by, but as he came closer, a man wearing a white suit, white shirt, and white tie came around the back waving his arms and stepped out into the road.

"Thank God above someone's come my way!" the man said in an Irish accent. "I'm having a devil of a time here, a devil of a time."

Joe might have kept riding except that the man was right in his way. An enticing aroma of cooking stew had reached his nostrils, giving him further motive to pause. There was a small cookfire burning a few yards off the road behind the wagon, a black kettle bubbling nicely with a coffeepot beside it.

"What's wrong?" Joe asked.

The man's expression of pleasure changed subtly for a moment, which told Joe he had just been recognized as an Indian. If the realization made much difference to the white-suited fellow, he didn't show it, for a moment later his expression was as before. He set up a busy chatter. "What's wrong, you ask? I'll tell you, sir, I'm on three wheels, that's what. Rolling right along, and there goes the hub, loose as a goose, so off I hop to try to fix it. But fixing a wagon wheel is a thing that I now know this Irish picture taker was not put into this world to do, for here now I sit with the wheel off and me not able to get it back on, and the jack's stuck tight besides. You look the sort who could put things right for me, if you will. Bless me, but I suppose I'd have sat here all night if you hadn't come."

Joe looked at the sky. "You might as well sit here all night anyway. It's late to start traveling again."

St. Patrick glanced around at the darkening land and lifted his arched brows. "Well, you're right about that. Too bad. I'd hoped to reach Hutchinson while the corpse was still fresh."

That comment intrigued Joe, but not nearly as much as the smell of the stew. "I'll fix your wheel for a bowl of that in the pot," he said.

"Why, if that's not a bargain, I've never run across one. Hop down there, friend, and see what you can do with that jack. The name's Pat St. Patrick."

Joe's mind scrambled for an alias. The best he could come up with was the one Tom Pease had given him the night of the shooting in the Indian Territory.

"My name is Henry Feather," Joe said.

"Good to meet you, Mr. Feather, good to meet you."

The wagon was easy enough to put right, and Joe had it done before it was fully dark. Then St. Patrick dished out stew in big crockery bowls, accompanied by mugs of coffee. Joe couldn't recall a better meal in months.

While they ate, St. Patrick talked incessantly, first about Ireland, then about his entry into the photographic business during the Civil War when he cut his professional teeth taking pictures of dead bodies on smoking battlefields. "I daresay that's what got me going in my specialty. Corpse photographs, I mean. Dead papas and mamas, and grandpas and newborns and such. Shutter off a clean close portrait, print it all up nice and neat, and stick it in a gilded frame, and you've got your dead relative in eternal repose right on the mantlepiece. That's what I do, and make a pretty penny at it. And then there's the outlaws. That's what I like best. Portraits of dead outlaws sell like bakery bread, they do. Especially when the bullet holes show."

Joe took a sip of his coffee and looked out across the plains, wondering if St. Patrick would talk all night. He was on the verge of rising to ride off to camp somewhere ahead when St. Patrick said something that made him decide to stay.

"Speaking of dead outlaws, Mr. Feather, it's to make a portrait of such a one that's got me in such a rush to get to Hutchinson. I got it from a firsthand witness this very morning that Caul Slidell himself has been gunned down by one of his own men just north of Hutchinson. I'm eager to make a picture of him before they get him planted."

Nothing in Joe Wolfkiller's impenetrable veneer changed to indicate the violent reaction St. Patrick's pronouncement generated. "Caul Slidell? You sure it was Slidell?"

"Well, the man who informed me of it said he saw it all happen himself, and he swore it to be Slidell. I intend to be the man who gets the last portrait of that scoundrel." St. Patrick cocked his head and looked at Joe's face by firelight. "Speaking of portraits, Mr. Feather, I'd like to ask if you'd consider letting me make one of you—all for free, of course, in thanks for fixing my wagon and for the evening's company. I find you an intriguing man; quite an imposing face and presence you have. Do I detect, uh, a certain Indian bloodline?"

"I'm who I am. Bloodlines don't matter."

St. Patrick waved his hand. "Oh, please take no offense, for none was intended. Anything I say is intended only in the highest and most complimentary sense. Now, about that portrait . . ."

"I have no use for a portrait."

St. Patrick looked disappointed. He poured himself another cup of coffee and started talking again, this time about childhood memories of Ireland—boyish explorations in places with names that meant nothing to Joe: Tralee Bay, Castle Gregory, Blennerville, Dingle, Listowell.

Joe shut it all out, his mind filled with questions about the reported death of Slidell. He hoped it was not true. If Slidell was already dead, Joe had lost both his chance at personal vengeance and his means of saving Will Ax. He brooded over the matter for a long time, then looked up and interrupted St. Patrick in midsentence. "If I let you make my picture, will you let me ride with you to Hutchinson to see this body?" he asked. Joe was not content with thirdhand word of Slidell's death. He wanted to see for himself.

St. Patrick, obviously surprised, grinned broadly. "Indeed, Mr. Feather, and thank you, sir. Thank you indeed."

Will Ax put down his volume of *Pilgrim's Progress* and took a deep breath. He had just reread one of his favorite portions—Christian's battle with Apollyon—but even that had failed to overcome the deep depression that had gripped him.

Why he was being held in this third-story room he did not know. Nor did he know what had become of Joe Wolfkiller. He feared for his young companion. Even now Joe might be in chains and heading for Parker's court in Arkansas.

Will Ax rose from his chair and walked stiffly over to the single narrow window. He looked out the dusty glass and over the weathered top of a roof that peaked at an impossibly steep angle. He had stared at that roof scores of times since being locked in here, trying to ascertain if he could hope to make it across to the lightning rod and clamber down without falling and breaking his neck. Several times he had almost tried; each time he had backed out. He was too old and feeble to do such a boyish thing, especially since the *ulunsuti* was gone. Its absence seemed to siphon much of his strength and will to try.

Given his unwillingness to attempt the roof route, the only alternative Will Ax had been able to think of was an old formula taught him by an uncle who swore that its words would allow him to take the form of a *tlayku*, a jaybird, and fly out of troublesome situations such as this. Will had chanted the long-memorized formula perfectly (he had noticed lately that for some reason it was easier to recall things he had learned long ago than things he had learned recently), but when he looked at his arms, they were still arms and not wings. After the first surge of disappointment he had decided that maybe he really was in the form of a jay but that to his eyes alone he looked the same. To test the theory, he called through the locked door until the man named Miller, who seemed to be some sort of employee or crony of the mysterious Jim Christmas, came grumbling up the stairs.

Miller opened the door and stuck in his head. "What is it now, old man?"

"Tell me, Mr. Miller, do I look like a man or a bird to you?"

Miller had sworn fiercely, threatened a beating if bothered with such stupidity again, then slammed and relocked the door. Will Ax had felt really dejected then, for he knew the old formula had not worked.

As much as he despised admitting it, it seemed that in the past few years a lot of old things, including the most venerable ancient formulas and even his precious *ulunsuti* stone, didn't work as they were supposed to. For that matter, Will Ax himself didn't work nearly as well as he had. His mind was slow, his body slower. Sometimes it hurt just to move; sometimes it hurt in a deeper way even to think.

Will Ax stood at the window looking out over that sharp roof peak at Christmas's backyard and the dirt road beyond it. He felt unwanted doubts trying to break out of the mental prison cells in which he had locked them for fear of facing them. The truth was, despite all his talk of being a magician, he had never really been able to achieve anything with his formulas that he could say wouldn't have happened anyway. Even his revered *ulunsuti* stone had never told him anything he could be sure was secret knowledge and not just some intuition or good guess. Back in his younger days, when the *ulunsuti* had reflected the light much more brightly than it did now, had been regularly "fed" with blood and correctly kept in a cave instead of a pocket, he had felt greater confidence in it. Perhaps his loss of confidence reflected a real change in the crystal—or a change in himself.

The more he thought about such things, the more Will Ax felt sad and forsaken. "I think I'm sinking in the Slough of Despond," he said aloud, making another reference to the "Pilgrim's Progress" allegory. He had made an instant mental shift from magician to Methodist, and without the slightest jolt. The process of jumping between two worldviews had become so practiced for Will Ax that he didn't notice anymore when he was doing it. He had discovered that contradictions weren't all that hard to live with if you put your mind to it—or more accurately, declined to let yourself think about it. Sometimes whole hordes of incompatible propositions would sit side by side in his mind, as comfortable with each other as old friends sharing pipes and memories.

Something on the road caught Will Ax's eye. A boy, walking slowly along and looking at Jim Christmas's house. He interested Will Ax. The lad was obviously a full-blood Indian. Will Ax's seasoned eye could tell that at this distance, even though the boy was dressed and trimmed up like a white youth. The old man proudly noted that at least his physical eyesight hadn't dulled along with its mystical counterpart. Just then the boy looked directly up at Will Ax's window, and Will waved at him.

Will Ax had figured the window would be too dusty and dark to allow the boy to see him and was surprised when the youth waved back. A burst of inspiration struck Will Ax, and he began a beckoning wave, trying to signal for the boy to climb up to him. The boy stopped walking and looked at Will Ax with a doubtful expression that slowly became fearful. He turned and darted away.

Will Ax was disappointed. He went to the bed and lay down. The day passed, and about seven o'clock Miller came up with a tray of food, grumbling about being forced to play "house slave to a wormy old redskin." Will Ax, assuming a stereotypical dime-novel talking style, told Miller that "red man heap pleased to have such good white slave," and Miller slapped him across the left cheek. The blow smarted, but Will Ax didn't much care. It had been worth it to insult Miller.

Miller took away Will Ax's plates before he had a chance to eat his fill and left the old man locked in the dark. Will Ax again lay down, wondering why he was held here, and slowly drifted off to sleep.

A scratching noise awakened him. It was very dark in the room now, obviously quite late. He sat up, looked around, and saw nothing. Perhaps it had been a mouse in the wall. The noise came again, and this time he was able to trace it. The window. He looked over, bleary-eyed from sleep, and thought with amazement that he saw a jay scratching the other side of the glass. He blinked and realized he had been wrong: It was not a jay but a small hand, the hand of a boy. And then he saw the face too, peering in, and recognized it as that of the Indian boy he had seen earlier.

Will Ax rose and went to the window. As quietly as possible, he opened it. "Come in, *tlayku*," he said. "Come in."

The boy thrust a leg through the window and entered. For several moments he looked up at Will Ax in undisguised awe. "Hello, Grandfather," he said in a whisper. He threw his arms around Will Ax and hugged him tight.

Chapter 8

"**My** name is Will Ax," the old man said haltingly, taken aback by the surprising affection with which the boy hugged him. The lad was about twelve years old. "And who are you, young *tlayku*?"

"My name is Timothy," the boy said softly. "Why do you call me—whatever that name was?"

"*Tlayku*. 'Jay,' in my language. I call you that because you must have become able to fly like a jay to reach me across this high roof."

"I didn't fly. I climbed. I'm a good climber, Grandfather."

"Now I have a question for you, Timothy. Why do you call me Grandfather?"

"Because you are so much like my grandfather—my real grandfather. He was a Creek."

"He is dead?"

"Yes. When I saw you through the window today, I thought Grandfather had come back to this world. At first I was scared . . . but I had to come back to see." The young boy saddened. "But I can see you are not really my grandfather."

"No. I am just an old Cherokee conjurer who is a prisoner in this room."

"A prisoner? Why?"

"I don't know, Timothy. I am held here by a man named Jim Christmas."

"Yes. This is his house. He is a rich man and, my father says, a bad one. He got rich from the railroad and

60

from buying and selling land. And he has cheated people, and that has made him richer. He makes friends of other people who have money and power and keeps them from knowing he's bad. That's what my father says."

"Your father, he is a Creek?"

"No. My Creek parents are dead. I've been with my white parents for six years. They are good to me... even though they'll thrash me if they find out I came here."

Will Ax smiled sadly. Timothy's situation made him think again of his lost daughter.

"May I still call you Grandfather, even if you are not really my grandfather?" the boy asked.

"Yes. It would make me proud. But while we talk here, we must keep our voices very low."

"Grandfather, if you are a Cherokee conjurer, why haven't you escaped?"

"Because, I'm afraid, I'm not a very good conjurer anymore. I'm old and not much good at anything except sleeping and making smoking pipes. And now that my *ulunsuti* stone is gone, it's even worse than before."

"What is an *ulunsuti* stone?"

Will Ax walked back over to the side of his bed and sat down. He lighted the single lamp beside his bed. By its light he got his first good look at Timothy, a small-framed but handsome boy.

"An *ulunsuti* stone is a powerful crystal, taken from the forehead of a fearsome beast called a Uktena. It is the greatest talisman a man can possess. For years it was mine, but now it belongs to a white man. Since it's gone, I—"

Will Ax cut off abruptly. Inspiration had struck him. He leaned forward. "Timothy, do you think you could enter another house as easily as you entered this one?"

"Yes."

"And as quietly?"

"Yes!"

Will Ax smiled. "Then you can do Grandfather a great favor and take back his *ulunsuti* for him."

"Where is it?"

"In a house belonging to a doctor who gives out bad-tasting medicine and doesn't much like Indians."

"Dr. Lansford."

"Yes, I believe that is his name."

"I know his house. I can get inside easy. Your stone is there?"

"Yes, and if you return it to me, I believe it would tell me how to escape this place."

Joe Wolfkiller stood like a statue in the morning light, staring out toward the horizon with a chiseled-stone expression until St. Patrick made his exposure and told him he could move. The halfbreed let out a breath and relaxed.

St. Patrick was in high spirits. "Very good, Mr. Feather! That should be excellent, just excellent."

Wordlessly, Joe turned away and headed off to saddle his horse. He cared nothing for the portrait; only to remain in St. Patrick's good graces had he agreed to have it made. Now he was eager to get on to Hutchinson and find out the truth about the report of Caul Slidell's death.

St. Patrick, who had been so anxious to reach Hutchinson the previous day, today was far too unhurried to suit Joe. St. Patrick dawdled as he put away his camera and devoted most of his energy to talking. "Gone are the old days of wet plates and rushing to develop them before the emulsion dries up," he said as he packed his gear. "Dry plates, Mr. Feather! Wonderful things. They take much of the rush out of this business. Thank God for bright sunshine and Eastman's Instantaneous! That's my motto."

When Joe's impatience was about to lead him to begin riding toward Hutchinson alone, St. Patrick at last finished loading his darkroom wagon. They set off, wheels creaking and squeaking, St. Patrick singing an old number about Galway Bay and "that little Irish girl of mine in the land of emerald green."

Once they reached Hutchinson, they had no difficulty finding the whereabouts of the corpse reputed to be Caul Slidell's. A gang of excited boys, accompanied by an even larger number of mongrel dogs, met St. Patrick's wagon at the edge of town, having noted the writing on the sideboards.

"You come to take pictures of Caul Slidell, huh?" "We'll take you there—just follow us." "You're going to show the holes in him, ain't you? I seen 'em, we all seen 'em—his chest looks like the top of a pepper box. It was a shotgun that killed him, you know!"

Joe felt exposed and out of place in Hutchinson, this white man's town in white man's country. He received some open stares from the boys who were steering St. Patrick through the streets. He hoped the people here would take him to be St. Patrick's assistant or employee and that the local law would not be looking too hard at the moment for Cherokee Joe.

The corpse was on ice in a storehouse located between a café and a wagon shop. The café owner seemed to be the recognized keeper of the body, for it was to his door that the crowd of boys ran.

The owner came out, wiping his hands on his apron. He beamed when he saw that a photographer had arrived. "Yes sir, I'd be proud for you to take a picture of our good Mr. Slidell," the man said after St. Patrick made his request. The fellow's name was Tarsus Castle, and he had a bald head and a nose that looked as if it had been mashed flat and pasted down. "And if you would, I'd like one with me standing right beside him. Something to keep for the grandchildren to have someday, you know."

"Indeed, indeed," said St. Patrick.

Joe stood to the side near the front of the growing crowd trying to appear inconspicuous but feeling very noticeable. Three men went into the storage house and came out with a blanket-wrapped body, now quite stiff. As soon as the cadaver was out the door, the mood of the crowd changed, dampering from vociferous excitement to hungry eagerness to see the gruesome body. Most of the people here had surely seen it earlier, Joe figured, but no one seemed less than eager to take a second look.

The body was on its back and bound to a wide board. After the knots were untied and the wrapping blanket loosened, Joe swallowed tensely and waited for the corpse to be unveiled, hoping it wouldn't be Slidell.

Tarsus Castle was about to pull the blanket away when four men on horseback came riding around the corner, generating enough ruckus and aura of importance to draw attention. Joe had a bad feeling about the new arrivals;

they had the smell of law about them. He pulled his hat a little lower over his eyes and made sure his long coat was draped fully over his gunbelt. He leaned so the pistol butt wouldn't make a visible bulge.

The lead rider dismounted lightly and walked through a gap in the crowd to Tarsus Castle and the body. His companions followed. St. Patrick, meanwhile, was just finishing setting up his camera directly in front of the body.

"Well, hello there, Sheriff," Castle said.

Sheriff! Joe looked down at his boots, letting the brim of his hat intercede between him and the peace officer.

"Hello, Tarsus. This must be the body in question?"

"Yes, sir. We iced him to keep him fresh until you could get back to see him. Just getting ready to get a picture made when you rode in." He waved over at St. Patrick.

"Yes, yes," said the sheriff. "Well, let's see him."

The crowd surged forward a little as Tarsus Castle pulled away the blanket. A ripple and murmur stirred through the group as they saw the whitish dead face, going blue around the mouth, the eyes half opened and glazed. The sheriff leaned over and looked closely at the dead face.

"Looks like Slidell to me," he said.

"That's him, all right," one of the deputies commented.

"He raved right up until the end about the robbery at the train station down in Guthrie," Castle said. "He lay right in my own house raving about it. Died right in my own bedroom." It was evident that Castle considered it a great honor to have played final host to an outlaw. "It was one of his own men that shot him. Left him for dead. I figured it was my duty to tend him until he passed."

"You're a good man, Tarsus," someone in the crowd said.

The sheriff turned to his deputies. "We'll make official notification, then: Caul Slidell was shot just outside Hutchinson and is officially verified as dead as of this date and time, etcetera and so on. You know the process."

Joe Wolfkiller was in turmoil. He had looked at the corpse and like all the others had at first thought it to be

Slidell, but a moment's further examination had shown that to be wrong. This blue-faced dead man was Ed Wiltflower, one of Slidell's hellriders. Wiltflower had always borne a resemblance to Slidell and sometimes had been confused with him in life. Now the same thing was happening in death.

Joe assessed the two possible results of the confusion. One was positive, one negative. The positive was that the real Slidell, once he learned he was now thought dead, would let down his guard and be more susceptible to capture. That could give Joe an edge he needed.

Then there was the negative. Word would surely reach Jim Christmas that Slidell was reported dead, and that would be disastrous for Will Ax. Will was useful to Christmas only as a means of keeping Joe on his leash until Slidell was brought in. If Christmas heard that Slidell was dead, he would have no more use for Joe and therefore no reason to keep Will Ax any longer. Maybe Christmas would set Will free, but Joe doubted it. Most likely he would put a bullet through the old man's brain and dump him out on the plains for the birds and scavengers.

Joe couldn't risk that happening. So despite the danger, he stepped forward.

"Sheriff."

The lawman turned around, frowning at the swarthy young stranger.

"That dead man . . . that's not Caul Slidell."

The sheriff's eyes were droopy and soft, roofed by brows that slanted up toward the crest of his forehead at nearly a forty-five degree angle. They tilted even more as he scanned Joe Wolfkiller up and down. Joe bristled under his gaze, feeling the rising fury that so often came when white eyes trailed over him like that.

"Who are you, redskin?"

Joe ignored the question. "That isn't Slidell," he reasserted. "I've seen this man before. His name is Ed Wiltflower."

"Wiltflower!" The sheriff looked around at his deputies and snorted. "What kind of name is Wiltflower?"

"That's his name," Joe said flatly.

The sheriff put a thick finger on Joe's chest. "Look

here, Injun, don't waste my time. I know what Slidell looks like. That's him on the board. Now, I suggest to you that you ride south down to the Nations where your kind belongs."

As Joe looked into the meaty face, anger flared in him like coals in a drafty oven. Such anger never went away for Joe; it only burned hotter or cooler, depending upon who or what had fanned it most recently. With wrenching effort, the halfbreed managed to restrain himself. He turned and walked off to the side, pulse pounding in his temples.

St. Patrick took his pictures, several of them, some of the corpse alone, others of the sheriff by its side, others including the proud Tarsus Castle.

Joe didn't watch. He stood alone, feeling he had failed. The body of Ed Wiltflower was being officially accepted as that of Caul Slidell. Telegraph wires would quickly carry the news across the Midwest. Jim Christmas would hear, and then...

Joe felt deeply depressed. Will Ax, crazy as he was, had been a good man to ride with. And it seemed awfully sad that he would die with his quest unfulfilled, his lost daughter never found.

Joe sat glumly on the back doorstep of Castle's café eating a bowl of beans with corn bread as he mused over the peculiar twists of the last few days.

St. Patrick, whose generosity was responsible for Joe's current meal, came around the café's back corner. He was bright and bubbly as ever. "Ah, there you are, Mr. Feather! Oh, what a day it's been, what a day! Excellent photographs they were, and sure to bring a good price. These I'll sell to the eastern papers, no question. But tell me, what were you saying to the sheriff about Slidell's body? I couldn't hear."

"I told him it wasn't Slidell," Joe said.

"Wasn't Slidell!" St. Patrick's face fell. "But it has to be Slidell—everyone said so."

"Everyone was wrong."

"How can you be sure? I would think a sheriff would know a wanted outlaw if he looked him in the face.

Speaking of wanted outlaws, do you know what I over-heard just now? I heard a man say the sheriff is all in a mad fury, declaring that Cherokee Joe is in town. Apparently he saw him on the street earlier and realized who he was when he went back to his desk and looked through his *wanted* posters."

Joe's now-empty bowl of beans slid from his lap to the ground. He was looking not at St. Patrick but at an upper window of the adjacent storehouse. His eyes narrowed. He had seen something there—a subtle motion, a shifting of the light . . .

"The sheriff has men out looking for Cherokee Joe right now. If he really is in town, I'm hoping they catch him. It would be a fine accomplishment indeed to add a portrait of Cherokee Joe to my portfolio."

Joe stood. "You already have," he said. Then he put his hand on St. Patrick's head and pushed him straight back. The photographer yelped once in surprise, then yelped again when a shot rang from the upper window of the storage building. A slug slammed into the wooden porch just where Joe had been seated a moment earlier. St. Patrick realized after sitting up that the halfbreed's pushing him back had put him well out of the line of fire.

Joe dived to the side as the next shot came. It was one of the deputies firing. He was a nervous and inaccurate rifleman, and a treacherous and cowardly one, firing from hiding as he was.

St. Patrick stood and backed up against the café wall, palms flat and eyes wide. He watched as the man he had known as Henry Feather yanked back the tail of his coat and drew out a well-oiled Colt Peacemaker in one smooth motion. The pistol cracked, and the man behind the window above screeched and disappeared into the store-house.

"By the saints!" the Irish portrait maker said. "You really are Cherokee Joe!"

Around the corner behind Joe came another man, carrying a scattergun. Joe wheeled and fired just as the newcomer blasted off a shot. The effort did him no good, for the entire load of buckshot missed Joe and ripped a hole in the white-painted back wall of Castle's café. St. Patrick, standing near the point of impact, yelled and took off at a run. Meanwhile, Joe's shot took the shotgunner in the shoulder and made him drop his weapon. The man gripped his wound; blood came between his fingers. He staggered back and out of sight.

The back door of the café swung open, and Tarsus Castle appeared, an old cap-and-ball Colt in his left hand. "What's going on here?" he bellowed.

Joe swung his pistol toward him. "Back inside!" he ordered.

Castle went pale, glanced down at the old pistol he held, tossed it aside as if it had suddenly gone hot in his hand, and ran back inside.

Joe darted behind the big storage building, hoping to find a back way to circle to his horse, tethered to a hitchrail on the street a few buildings down. A man appeared before him, coming from the end of an alley. Joe fired. The man clutched his midsection and fell to his knees—the sheriff himself. He wavered and pitched forward. Joe had no chance to see if he was dead, for he heard others running up the alleys on both sides of the building. Lacking any other option, he ducked into the rear door of the storage house.

Inside, Ed Wiltflower's corpse still lay on ice in a big wooden box on two sawhorses. Joe leaped it, heading for the stairs. The toe of his boot caught the corner of the box and tipped it over. The blue-faced cadaver fell out, ice chunks sliding across the floor. Joe ran up the stairs.

He had forgotten the gunman who had fired down at him from the window of this building—forgotten, that is, until he saw him again.

He was lying in the corner bleeding from a wound on his neck. He stared at Joe in utter fear, his face white. "Don't kill me!" he pleaded. "Don't kill me, please!"

Joe kicked the gun out of the deputy's limp hand. It clattered across the floor and struck the wall. "Why shouldn't I kill you?" he said. "You tried to murder me from hiding."

The wounded man had no answer. His eyes went big and bright, and then he fainted, sinking into darkness and no doubt expecting never to reemerge. Joe saw now that the man's neck wound was hardly more than a bloody scratch and felt contempt for the fellow.

Joe scanned the room for a way out. He hoped for a ladder to the roof, a walkway across to an adjacent building, any escape route. But there was none. And now he heard men entering the room below him, exclaiming as they found the overturned box and the body on the floor.

"Upstairs!" one shouted. "He's upstairs!"

Their feet pounded loudly on the steps.

Chapter 9

When he traveled to Guthrie in the Indian Territory a few weeks later to photograph the first land run and make a property claim for himself on the side, Pat St. Patrick would talk expansively and proudly of how he watched Cherokee Joe make his incredible escape from Hutchinson, Kansas. He would keep talking of it for the rest of his life, which he mostly spent in the little Guthrie photographic studio he established. As he talked, he would show off the photograph that made him famous: Cherokee Joe himself, long coat draped to hide his gun as he posed stiffly on a roadside, staring into the Kansas morning sunlight.

Some years later, St. Patrick would print his recollection of Cherokee Joe's flight for life. The story, first printed privately in Guthrie and then in a newspaper in Wichita, would be published by other newspapers and finally across the nation.

The story would tell of his chance meeting with "Henry Feather" on the road to Hutchinson and the young man's aid in fixing the wagon. "Though I did not know my new companion, I could tell even then the young man had in him a dark secretiveness, a secretiveness as dark as his swarthy skin," St. Patrick wrote, giving himself credit for a foresight he had not possessed. "I suspected him at once of being an Indian in northward flight from the Nations for some trouble or another that had come his way, though never in my most lurid imaginings did I then consider that this might be the feared Cherokee Joe Wolfkiller, whose infamy even at that moment was spreading like a fire across the plains because of his dramatic gunning down of peace officers on the plains of the Nations."

Such verbosity would be skipped over by many readers, who would scan directly to the most exciting part—St. Patrick's description of Cherokee Joe's escape from the upper level of the storage house where he was finally cornered.

St. Patrick: "There I stood on that earthen street, shaken to my heart, nay, my soul, by the violence I had witnessed. I knew that my former companion was now trapped in the upper floor of that building, for I had seen a half dozen armed men converge upon it and enter. I waited in grim expectation for the gunshot that would mark the end of Cherokee Joe's life, and as was my anticipation, a shot rang out, muffled by the walls of the building. No sooner had I lowered my head to voice a quick prayer for the heathen's soul than did the single front and upper window of the storage house explode outward, and through it come the form of the man I had assumed had just been killed.

"It was, indeed, Cherokee Joe, very much alive, with pistol in hand and long coat trailing in high dramatic fashion behind his slender form. Onto the roof of the porch of his former prison he had leaped. He darted to his right, then upon seemingly changing his mind, left again, discharging his Colt pistol back through the shattered window as he passed. That shot, I was later informed, sadly took the life of an innocent man, named B. N. Smith, who had joined the peace officers in their pursuit of the fearsome halfbreed.

"From the porch roof Cherokee Joe made a leap most impressive, flying through the air a remarkable distance to the slightly lower porch roof on a building adjacent. From this perch, clearly, he intended to make his descent to the ground and race to his nearby horse, but the sudden appearance below of another armed man intent upon his capture forced him to remain where he was. He moved down the roof approximately ten feet and then climbed to the rooftop, dropping over the high falsefront that then hid him from my sight for the span of fifteen seconds.

"He emerged next on the ground, holding before him a young woman around whose neck his arm was tightly crooked. He had taken his hostage, I later learned, from the back door of a dress shop—the poor maiden had stepped out to see what was causing all the commotion. As he advanced toward his horse, he alternately held his pistol to her head and waved it generally at all his observers, ordering all the while that he be allowed to escape or the unfortunate young woman would pay with her life. In this manner he reached his horse. He was forced to release the girl in order to mount, and she ran quickly to the relative safety of the other side of the street. A great explosion of gunfire immediately erupted from the pursuers who were now emerging again onto the street, but Cherokee Joe escaped the borders of the town without harm, a feat later attributed by one local preacher to a miracle of devils. Whatever its nature, the escape had the effect, so common in cases of this sort, of making Cherokee Joe something of a dashing and heroic figure in the eyes of many, including those old and intelligent enough to know better."

Including, had he been honest enough to say it, Pat St. Patrick, who for the rest of his life did more than any other man to keep the legend of Cherokee Joe alive and thriving.

When the night came again to Will Ax, so also came the Creek boy named Timothy. The old Cherokee, who had been seated on his bed anxiously waiting, helped him to enter.

"Timothy, did you—"

"It was easy, Grandfather," Timothy said as he held out his small brown hand. "I waited until Dr. Lansford was in his office downstairs and climbed up his trellis to the window. I had to break the glass to reach the lock, but no one heard me, and no one saw me. The crystal was on the table beside his bed."

Will Ax took the little pouch from the boy's hand, opened it, took out the *ulunsuti* stone, and cupped it in his palm. He closed his eyes and squeezed his treasure lovingly, then opened them and touched the boy's shoulder. "You have made me complete again, Timothy. Now I will find the way to escape this place."

"When you do, will you come and visit me?"

"If I can, I will. If I can't, you can know that I am always grateful to you and will see you when we both are in the Celestial City." Will Ax turned his head suddenly. "Go now—I hear someone coming."

Scarcely had Timothy slipped out the window when the door rattled and opened. Miller thrust in his head. "Who you talking to up here, old man?"

"To myself. I have been giving myself wise counsel, telling myself I should be more grateful to my fine hosts for the hospitality they have shown an old Indian."

"Well, do your wise counseling during the daytime— else maybe we won't be such good hosts anymore."

"Thank you, friend Miller. Your counsel is even wiser than my own."

The lamp in Miller's hand sent flickering light into the room; some of it glinted with surprising brilliance on the *ulunsuti* stone in Will Ax's hand.

"What's that you got there?" Miller asked, stepping in.

Will Ax knew that to hide the *ulunsuti* would only ensure it being taken from him, so he held it out for Miller to see. "It is only a piece of quartz stone," he said. "Just a pretty rock."

Miller was suspicious. "Let me see that. I never seen a quartz flash that bright."

Will Ax did not let his dismay show as he laid the *ulunsuti* stone in Miller's hand. The ugly little man held it up and examined it in the lamplight. In his fingers it did not seem the bright thing it had been in Will Ax's hand; it glinted dully like any piece of quartz.

"Huh," Miller said grumpily, thrusting the stone back at Will Ax. "Thought you was keeping something from me there, old man. Thought you had a diamond or some such."

He turned and left the room. Will Ax took a deep breath. He put the crystal back into its hide wrapping and put the package under his pillow, then went to the dark window and looked out. "May your pilgrimage be safe and all your quests successful, Timothy," he whispered.

He climbed into his bed. When he slept, his dreams were peaceful and full of renewed confidence.

The rattle and squeak of an approaching wagon awakened Will Ax early the next morning. He got out of bed and went to the window. A large freight wagon pulled by a team of mules had rumbled up to the front door. Jim Christmas emerged and talked to the driver, who then pulled the wagon around the far side of the house out of Will's sight.

The aging Cherokee stretched and yawned, and noted happily to himself that he felt stronger and younger today than he had in a long time. He took the *ulunsuti* from beneath his pillow and examined it again. "Today we will escape," he said to it.

Miller later brought up Will Ax's breakfast—toasted bread and eggs on a heavy china plate. "Tell me, friend Miller, does Mr. Christmas own you like I own my piece of quartz?" Will Ax asked. He knew the question would anger Miller, but he felt feisty today.

Miller swore at him and left, slamming the door hard. When he returned for the plate, Will Ax was standing where the door would hide him when it opened. Miller thrust his head in. Will Ax came around and smashed the china plate down on his skull. Miller fell unconscious.

Will Ax beamed. He dragged Miller farther into the room and rifled his pockets. He found a small amount of cash, some twist tobacco, and a loaded pocket pistol. Putting the items into his coat, he stepped across the prone form. "Thank you for all your kindness," he said to Miller.

Miller groaned and started to stir. Will Ax picked up half the china plate and knocked him cold once more.

Will Ax slipped into the hallway and crept along as quietly as he could. He heard movement, and thinking someone was about to mount the stairs, ducked into the next room, another bedroom. He heard voices from below. Near the fireplace a ventilation grate was cut through the floor to allow heat from the iron stove below to rise to the upper level.

Will Ax went to the grate and looked down. Jim Christmas stood, coffee cup in hand, talking to the man who had driven the freight wagon. Will Ax heard that the wagon was loaded with plow parts and other farming equipment picked up from a warehouse in Wichita. Christmas, he gathered, had sold the items to a merchant some miles to the north and was delivering them by wagon because of some foul-up at the railroad freight yard.

Such talk was of no interest to Will Ax, but he lingered anyway, trying to figure out the layout of the house from what he could see and remember. It appeared he would have to make it past the door of the room Christmas was in if he was to find an exit. Could he do it without being seen?

He was about to try when the conversation below took a new angle that caught his attention and stopped him. The man with Christmas asked, "What you intend to do about Slidell, Jim?"

"Slidell is being dealt with," Christmas said. "And you'd never guess how."

"The truth is, I know a little about it already," the man said. "Miller told me you somehow got Cherokee Joe himself to go after him."

"He told you that, huh? Miller talks too much. But that's right. The halfbreed turned up out in the shed, hiding out from a storm with an old Indian codger. I tell you, it was a gift from Providence. Now I have the old Indian locked upstairs—a hostage, you know, to make sure Cherokee Joe brings Slidell back. I'll set things square with Caul Slidell as soon as I get my hands around his double-crossing neck. Kind of funny how it worked out because Cherokee Joe was already going after Slidell for murdering his father. That's another bone I've got to pick with Slidell. He had no reason to clutter up our carefully planned robbery with the murder of those Indians."

"I ain't worried about no lousy dead Indians," said the other man. "I worry about getting our cut of those jewels back from Slidell."

"We'll get them back, never fear. I'll carve them out of his hide if it comes to that."

"You really think Cherokee Joe will bring him back?"

"I do. He seems very attached to that old red coon upstairs. He won't let harm come to him."

Will Ax smiled. He was touched to hear of Joe's devotion. At the same time he felt a mounting sense of alarm. Now he understood why he had been kept a prisoner and what had happened to Joe Wolfkiller.

"Is Slidell still up beyond Great Bend?" the other man asked.

"As far as I know, yes. That's where I sent the halfbreed."

"Well, if there's any who can haul in Slidell, it'd be the likes of Cherokee Joe. I hear he's a fierce one."

"He's just another angry Indian who happens to be a little angrier than most," Christmas said. "When he comes back, I'll take delivery of Slidell, put a quick slug through Cherokee Joe's skull, and ship his corpse off to Parker for a present." He chuckled.

The men left the room. Will Ax followed the sound of their voices farther back into the house. Now was the moment for escape, now before they came back, before Miller regained consciousness in the next room. He headed down the stairs as lightly as he could. He was tense but unusually alert and confident. He was on top of his situation again. He had his *ulunsuti*, his *Pilgrim's Progress*, and a gun. Nothing could stop him now.

He made it out of the house and headed for the road. He peered around a corner of the house and saw the loaded wagon. He crept around it, and then a side door of the house opened. The voice of Jim Christmas wafted over. Will Ax panicked and looked wildly for a place to hide.

The wagon pulled out a couple of minutes later. Christmas said goodbye to the driver and wished him luck on his delivery, then wondered aloud where Miller had gone for so long. The other said he didn't know and didn't much care because he thought Miller was an irritating little squat anyway.

The wagon creaked off. Hidden among the crates and

plow parts, beneath the tarpaulin spread across it all, Will Ax grinned. He thought it funny and ironic that Christmas's cargo wagon had turned into his vehicle of escape.

Will Ax was eager to get back to his quest to find his daughter, but for now he would have to lay that aside to take up a more pressing matter. He had to find Joe Wolfkiller and tell him he had escaped, that Jim Christmas no longer was a threat to either of them. He did not know how he would find Joe... unless the crystal could help him.

He pulled the *ulunsuti* from his pocket and by the sunlight seeping in around the edge of the tarpaulin looked deeply into its crystalline facets. This time, he hoped intensely, the stone would not keep silent. This time it could not, or he might never find Joe Wolfkiller.

The wagon jolted along, heading northwest across the rolling land.

Chapter 10

J oe Wolfkiller slipped the smoking pistol back into its holster and looked sadly at the horse he had just shot to death. There had been no choice; the horse had broken a front leg so thoroughly that the fractured bone protruded through the flesh. An unseen hole had caused the accident, which had tumbled Joe to the earth so hard the breath had been knocked out of him for several moments.

Now he was on foot, the worst situation for a man fleeing the law on the plains. There was no question that he would be pursued; the shoot-out in Hutchinson had been a horrific one. If Cherokee Joe had coveted fame as an outlaw, he had certainly found it.

It couldn't have come at a more inconvenient time.

He took his rifle from the saddle and began walking. It was a terrible feeling to be bound to a speed no greater than he could walk or run. And to be captured would be certain death, either on the spot or on the gallows.

He walked a long time until he was tired and sweating, despite the cool temperature. A sound caught his ear, coming over the hump of land ahead: the whistle of a train running northwest on the Atchison, Topeka, and Santa Fe rails.

Joe stopped for a moment thinking, then with a new burst of hope took off at a trot up the rise.

Will Ax's old bones were getting sore from the jolting the wagon was giving him. The driver had also taken to singing, and that was equally rough on Will's ears. Furthermore, the *ulunsuti* was being stubborn again and would not reveal anything about the whereabouts of Joe Wolfkiller no matter how intently Will Ax looked into it.

Will Ax had long ago come to think of his crystal as a personality (one much like himself) and at the moment was peeved at it. The ungrateful *ulunsuti* was simply being ornery, like a foul-tempered old goat, refusing to help when needed the most. Will finally tucked the crystal away in his pocket with disgust. As time passed and he thought about it more, he began to feel differently. Maybe the *ulunsuti* wasn't unwilling to help. Maybe it was just too weak.

A feeling of irresponsibility descended upon Will Ax. He knew he had not taken care of the *ulunsuti* as he should. A man as versed in the old lore as he had no excuse for not following the rules. An *ulunsuti* required a rubbing with the blood of a small-game animal at least every seven days and the blood of some larger animal about twice a year. And its home should be a hidden cave, not the pocket of a tattered old Union coat. Will Ax felt chagrined. The *ulunsuti*'s lack of responsiveness was probably his fault.

He realized he was fortunate that the *ulunsuti* had let him get away with such carelessness. According to the old stories, an *ulunsuti* improperly cared for changed to a flame by night and took the blood of its mishandler or one of his kin to replace what had been denied it. Yet no such revenge had befallen Will Ax, and since he had no kin left, it couldn't have befallen anyone else either. He was lucky.

A frightening thought suddenly came. He was wrong to think he had no remaining kin. He had kin in the daughter he was even now seeking, so long gone from him that he often failed to remember her as his own flesh. What if the stone had taken its revenge upon her, wherever she was? Will's heart beat faster, harder. His mouth began to go dry.

He reached into his pocket, pulled out the crystal again, and unwrapped it. "I am sorry I've neglected you," he whispered. "I will do better and feed you with blood as soon as I can." He began to fold the pouch around the crystal again, then stopped. "But I will tell you, talisman: If I find harm has come to my daughter because of you, I will smash you to pieces with a hammer."

He put the crystal away, wondering if he had been prudent to threaten it. He set his jaw. Prudent or not, he was glad he had done it. Sometimes the Methodist side of him made him antagonistic toward the conjurer side.

His thoughts were interrupted when the wagon gave a huge heave that threw Will Ax bodily off the wagonbed. The tailgate fell, and a crate beside him slid out from beneath the tarpaulin and crashed onto the ground. Will Ax barely retained his perch in the wagon.

He huddled down under the tarpaulin as he heard the driver curse and pull the wagon to a halt. In a moment he would be discovered, and there was no way to escape it.

Upon topping the rise, Joe Wolfkiller was surprised and pleased to see the train he had heard pull to a full stop below. He quickly saw why: Smoke was pouring out around one of the wheels of a freight car. The engineer and crew were spilling out of the engine cab and running back toward the smoking wheel, a brakeman coming around the other end of the train to join them.

Joe grinned. The train would be stopped for some time as the trainmen repacked the bearings in the overheated wheel journal. If Joe was lucky, he might be able to find a way to slip into one of the freight cars while they were distracted.

He made a wide circle around the train for fifteen minutes; he wanted to approach from the rear to minimize the angles from which he could be seen. The full attention of the crew would be on the repairs, he figured. His biggest problem would be finding a way inside a freight car. He reached the train near its end on the side opposite the area under repair, then stopped, looking up hopelessly at the big closed doors. Even if they weren't locked, he doubted he could open one without attracting the attention of someone on the crew.

He was startled when one of the doors on the next car down slid open as if of its own accord. Joe threw himself up against the side of the train and watched as a man came flying from the open door to sprawl on the ground. The trainman who had just booted him out stuck out his head. Joe caught a warning not to try to freeload on the railroad again. The trainman watched the man stomp off to begin his long and lonely walk to the nearest town, miles away, then pulled his head back inside—and did not close the door.

Joe could hardly believe his good fortune. He crept to the open car and looked inside. The door on the opposite side was also cracked open. The trainman had apparently heard movement inside the car after the stop and entered from the opposite side to investigate. He had now left the same way he had come and was talking and laughing with his fellow crew members at the repair site, describing how he had tossed off the freeloader.

Joe climbed in quietly and looked around the jumble of crates, boxes, and shapeless tarpaulin-draped freight items. He clambered onto some of the crates and headed toward the back corner. A space between two crates provided just enough room for him to sit down.

Only now did he have time to reflect on what had happened back in Hutchinson. How many men had he killed or wounded? He didn't know; he remembered the entire incident only as a disturbing blur of running, shooting, and fearing. Mostly fearing... but not as much as before.

It had been a little easier this time for Cherokee Joe to kill.

But only a little easier. As he sat waiting for the train to move, the fear came back and brought new ones with it. What if a posse overtook the stalled train and searched it? What if he found the law waiting for him wherever this train finally stopped? He was out of his home area now, away from the familiar plains of the Territory. This was Kansas, white men's country, crisscrossed by railroads and full of towns, farms, and people among whom he stood out like a cinder in a snow pile.

Joe jerked his head up and gasped through his teeth when he heard one of the big sliding doors slam shut and latch. The meager light in the freight car diminished by half. The other door slammed moments later, and it became as dark as late dusk. Joe closed his eyes, feeling a little safer behind hiding walls.

The train chugged and lurched and began moving again, picking up speed. The multi-branched Atchison, Topeka, and Santa Fe track ran a long way, passing through Larned, Kinsley, Dodge City, Cimarron, and many other towns. But first it passed through Great Bend, and that was as far as Joe needed to go, for it was near Great Bend that Caul Slidell and his hellriders were said to be holed up.

Knowledge of the task before him was daunting. Now it was even more complicated than before, for every telegraph wire was probably already singing with news of the terrible fight in Hutchinson. Alerts would be out. How could he hope to search down Caul Slidell when every law dog in Kansas was on his tail? It astounded Joe when he realized that his reputation might overshadow that of Slidell at the moment. He had gunned down men in the Territory and in Hutchinson. Some had been officers of the court.

It came to Cherokee Joe that men who did the things he had done usually lived short lives, and the thought gnarled his stomach. Despite the many times he had told himself that he did not fear death and would rather die young, rebellious, and vengeful, it had all been hypothetical talk. Now it was likely. Maybe a certainty.

Joe pulled out the little knife he always kept in a sheath inside his left boot, removed his hat, and hacked off his hair by the handfuls. He was desperate to change his appearance, to do anything to increase his chances of survival.

When he was through, he put the knife back in his pocket and his hat back on his head. He closed his eyes and noted that his head was pounding. The train rumbled along mesmerizingly. He slept and dreamed of Parker's gibbet and Maledon's noose.

Will Ax came out of the back of the wagon with a scream worthy of a panther. The driver, who had just tossed back the tarpaulin so he could put the fallen crate back in place, screamed just as impressively and fell back

on his rump, staring up in abject fright. Will Ax reached
into the big pocket in his coat and brought out his heavy
volume of *Pilgrim's Progress*. He raised it and pounded it
as hard as he could on the driver's head three times in
succession, then hammered a fourth blow square across his
face. The driver's eyes rolled up, and he fell back, blood
pouring from his broken nose.

Will Ax smiled and glanced up at the sky. "Thank you,
Mr. Bunyan," he said. "Your book has again been a benefit
to me."

The driver carried a Remington pistol, and Will Ax
took it. The gunbelt was too big to fit Will's thin waist, so
he draped it over one shoulder like a Mexican bandolier.
Now he had not only the little derringer he had taken from
Miller but a large side arm as well. He stood proudly,
feeling that with such armament he cut a fine and invinci-
ble figure.

The sight of the blood on the unconscious driver's
face gave Will Ax an idea. He pulled the *ulunsuti* from his
pocket, unwrapped it, and dabbled a good amount of
blood on it. "I don't know if white man's blood will serve
in place of an animal's, but it seems a good trade to me,"
he said to the crystal. "I hope this will make you strong
again and take away any anger you have against me."

Will Ax pulled off the tarpaulin and spread it over the
unconscious man. "I don't want you to get too cold sleeping on the ground," he said. "Such a thing isn't healthy. I
have nothing against you, and you did give me a fine
wagon ride." He climbed onto the wagon seat, pulled it
forward a little, and began scooting the wagon's contents
toward the back and onto the ground. It was hard work for
an old man and left him winded, but when he was done,
the wagon was lighter and fit for faster travel.

"Tell Mr. Christmas I'm sorry I stole his wagon, and
Mr. Miller that I am sorry I broke his china plate," Will Ax
said to the senseless figure. Then he climbed onto the
driver's seat again and set off.

Cherokee Joe awakened suddenly and opened his
eyes. He did not know for a moment where he was or why
he was in gray semidarkness and in motion. His head

cleared slowly, and he remembered that he was on the train. Out of instinct, he reached to check his guns.

And found them gone.

Joe stood, amazed and horrified. His guns couldn't be missing—his pistol had been in his belt, his rifle in his hand.

Then he knew he was not alone. He lifted his eyes. A man sat on a crate across from and slightly above him, a big fellow, white, scruffy-bearded, and very familiar. In his possession were Joe's rifle and pistol.

"Hello, Joe," he said.

"Hello, Hambone." Grogginess and tension had Joe feeling as if he were in the midst of a none-too-pleasant dream. "What are you doing here?"

"I was just getting ready to ask you the same thing," said Hambone Coltrane.

"I'm running from the law," Joe said. "I killed some men in the Territory and some more in Hutchinson."

"Hutchinson! Dang, Joe, you been busy! I'd heard about them deputies down in the Territory—everybody's heard about that by now—but I hadn't heard nothing about Hutchinson. When'd you do that one?"

Joe's sense of time was scrambled, so it took a few moments for him to remember. "This morning... if this is still today."

Hambone laughed. "Listen at you! You sound drunk, Joe."

"I'm not drunk." Joe rubbed his head. "What are you doing here? How'd you get on this train?"

"I got on pretty much the same way you did, and for pretty much the same reason. Me and an old boy name of Billy Spratlock got ourself into trouble down at Shadrah Camp's post. Billy and me went over for a little liquor, and I seen that old mule I give you back in the lot. I got to pining for it and wound up trying to steal it back, and it didn't quite work out. To make a long story short, I stuck a knife into Camp's shoulder, and me and Billy rode off on a couple of Camp's horses. That's when we decided it might be good to hitch us a train ride up into Kansas for a while, till things settled down a bit, you know. We slid ourselves into this here freight car, but dang if one of them railroad men didn't find Billy and toss him off back yonder. I was better hid, and he didn't find me. I heard you climb in, Joe, though I didn't know it was you till I crawled out and saw you sleeping here."

"Now you know," Joe said. "Give me my guns back, Hambone."

"No can do, Joe, no can do. You're my prisner, I'm sorry to tell you."

Joe glared at Coltrane in disbelief.

"It's just that I figure you're worth a whole lot, Joe. Not only in money but to help get me out of what trouble I'm in too." He flashed an apologetic smile. "I'm right sorry—you know how it is. Hey, you had any food?"

"Not since this morning."

"You're in luck, then. I got a big old hunk of corn bread I'll be happy to share with you."

The corn bread was dry and made Joe even thirstier than he already was. Still, he ate it to the last crumb. Coltrane munched his more slowly and with his free hand kept the pistol aimed at Joe's chest.

"You can't do this to me, Hambone," Joe said. "They'll hang me."

"Like I said, Joe, I'm sorry. By the way, what happened to your hair?"

"I cut it off."

"Did you now! Trying to change your looks, huh?"

"That's right."

Hambone Coltrane took another bite of corn bread. He chewed it slowly—and stopped suddenly. "What'd you cut that hair with, anyway?"

"With this." Joe came up as swift as a cat, lunged forward with the boot knife in his right hand, and cut a big slash across the hand of Hambone Coltrane. The big man yelped, jumped up, and dropped the pistol.

Chapter 11

Joe had the pistol in his hand an instant after it had thunked to the floor of the freight car. He expected Coltrane to swing around and grab for the rifle he had laid on a box behind him, but the porcine fellow lurched forward, grabbing at his throat. His eyes grew wide and wet, and he seemed to be trying to talk, though no sound came out.

Joe sheathed his knife, reached up behind Coltrane and took the rifle. "That dry corn bread's bad for choking a man," he said.

Hambone Coltrane stood, his fat legs bowed to either side and his hands at his throat. Joe holstered his pistol as he watched the big man choke. Serves him right, Joe thought. If he strangles on his own corn bread, it will be one of those rare cases of justice in an unjust world.

Then Coltrane fell to his knees. His watering eyes looked up pleadingly at Joe, and the halfbreed sighed. "All right, Hambone, all right." He turned the rifle butt forward and jammed the buttplate hard into Coltrane's diaphragm.

A sodden crust of corn bread came flying out of Coltrane's mouth. The big man sucked in the most welcome breath of his life as he sank to the floor.

"First time I ever whipped a man in a fight by choking him on corn bread. I should have let you strangle," Joe muttered as he stepped past Coltrane and made his way through the piles of cargo toward the center of the car.

He opened one of the doors a couple of feet and looked out. Nothing in the passing landscape gave him any hint of where he was. He wondered how long he should remain on the train. It seemed likely that by now news of what had happened in Hutchinson had been wired to every town and station along every rail line. The law would probably be on the alert for him wherever he went. He couldn't afford to be caught in a railroad car. And this car wasn't a pleasant place to be anymore with Hambone Coltrane along. Joe decided to jump, but first he pulled his head back in to make sure Coltrane was still in his place and prepare himself for what would be a rough tumble to the ground.

Coltrane was right behind him. He had crept up silently. A big fist swung out and pounded Joe's jaw. Joe was knocked out the open door. Instinctively he dropped his rifle and grabbed for a handhold to keep from falling out. Coltrane kicked the rifle away and chortled.

Joe let go with one hand and reached for his pistol. Coltrane, his face red, managed to grip the wrist of Joe's gunhand. Coltrane was as strong as he was big, and Joe could not level the pistol to fire. He was trapped in a deadly position, his entire body leaning back out of the speeding freight car, the toes of his boots barely retaining a hold on the edge of the floor.

"I'm still going to take you in, Joe!" Coltrane said through his gritted mossy teeth. "Give me that pistol or I'll snap your arm!"

Joe's entire arm was racked with pain as Coltrane began to twist it. The clinging fingers of his other hand began to slip from the edge of the door, which was beginning to slide away from him, making him even more unbalanced. His gunhand became weak; the gun fell, landing half in and half out of the car.

Coltrane reached down and grabbed it with his free hand, retaining his hold on Joe's arm. In the process he unwittingly wrenched Joe's arm even further, and the pain was more than Joe could take.

He let go of the car and fell straight back with an involuntary yell. For a moment Coltrane kept his grip, and Joe dangled in the air by his wrenched arm. Then he fell.

He couldn't have found a poorer place to drop. Beside the track lay the badly broken skeleton of a dog that had come to the end of its days under a train weeks before. Joe landed right atop it, and a sharp upthrusting shard of bone gashed his left arm painfully. He rolled down the embankment and lay gasping in the dirt and gravel.

Twisting his head, he watched the train pass, Coltrane's head sticking out of the car. He watched Joe until the train made a curve and his line of sight was cut off. Joe swore and stood, gripping his bleeding arm. A broken piece of dog bone was sticking out of it. He pulled it out with a shudder and dug into the back pocket of his denim pants for a bandanna, which he pressed tightly around his cut.

"Next time, Hambone...next time I let you choke!" Joe yelled at the disappearing train.

He sat down and collected his thoughts. He had wanted to leave the train, but not at the cost of a painful and infection-prone injury and not without his weapons. All he had now was his little boot knife. And he didn't even know where he was.

The sun was in the western half of the sky. Joe wondered if by dark he could find a place to sleep and steal some food and a horse. He had his doubts. Luck seemed to have left him the moment he awoke and saw Hambone Coltrane's ugly face.

Pressing the bandanna tighter, Joe staunched the flow of blood from the gash in his arm. His hat lay on the ground beside him. He picked it up, plopped it onto his raggedly shorn head, and began trudging along the side of the tracks.

Will Ax was nearly in despair by the time his commandeered wagon rolled into sight of Hutchinson the next morning. After stopping for the night along the road, he had consulted the *ulunsuti,* and from it he had gained no intuitions. The crystal felt heavy and cold and dead in his hand.

It had been a mistake, he decided, to bathe it in the blood of a white man. How could he have been so foolish?

He might have rendered the *ulunsuti* useless forever by exposing it to so alien a substance. "I've killed you, old friend, I've killed you," Will mourned. "Now I have nothing to give to my daughter before I die."

Will Ax was so hungry that he knew he would have to go into Hutchinson and see if he could find any white folks friendly enough to give some food to an aging Indian. After the team had eaten more grain, the Cherokee climbed on the wagon again and rolled into town.

He found the place in a state of excitement. He had expected to receive many curious and cold looks when he entered town—white folks usually acted that way toward Indians—but he had not expected the hostility he detected in every stare aimed his way. He pulled up the wagon in front of a café and climbed down stiffly.

He knew better than to go to the front door, so circled around to the back. Three men were there in a line with their backs toward him. One of them wore an apron. The others were nondescript, typical plains townsmen. All were standing stiff and straight as telegraph poles.

A fourth man was in front of them, behind a camera. When Will Ax came into view behind the men, the man lifted his head and glowered at him. "You're in the way, old fellow," Pat St. Patrick said. There was nothing unfriendly in his tone.

"I'm very sorry," Will Ax muttered. He backed up. St. Patrick took the picture and nodded at the men. They relaxed and broke line.

The one in the apron turned to Will Ax. "What are you doing here?" he asked. It was Tarsus Castle, the café owner.

"I came hoping to find someone willing to give a hungry Methodist some food," Will Ax said, trying to look very sad. White people, he had learned during his years of begging gifts from the cattlemen who trailed through the Indian Nations, often saw sad-looking Indians in a romanticized and tragic light that made them more generous.

"Methodist, huh?" Castle chuckled and looked at the others. "Hear that? This one's a Methodist." Castle's grin faded when he looked back at Will Ax. "You'll have to pardon me if I don't act too nice toward your kind today.

The last redskin we had in this town sure wasn't no Methodist. He left us with some new widows, one of them the sheriff's wife."

Will Ax didn't understand but sought no clarification. Overly inquisitive Indians were not popular among whites. "I'll go somewhere else," he said.

"That's the best idea you'll ever have, old man," Castle replied. He turned to St. Patrick. "You'll make sure I get a copy of that?"

"Indeed."

Castle gave Will Ax one more sour look and disappeared into his café through the back door. The other two subjects strode away through the alley up to the street.

Will Ax turned to follow, but St. Patrick said, "Wait, old fellow. Talk to me a minute."

Will Ax turned. "If you want."

"What kind of Indian are you?"

"Cherokee." He added proudly, "I'm a conjurer."

"You don't say! You look like you could stand to conjure up some food at the moment."

Will Ax's stomach answered with a well-timed growl.

"I'll make a bargain with you, Mr. . . ."

"Ax." Will Ax liked the ring of "mister." He seldom was granted such dignities.

"Mr. Ax. I'll buy you something to eat if you'll allow me to make your portrait."

"My portrait?" Will Ax's ego rose to a new height. "Yes. Thank you, sir."

"Pat's the name. Call me Pat."

St. Patrick went into Castle's café and emerged with a tray piled with food—hot eggs, biscuits, coffee, bacon, bread soaked in molasses. Will Ax sat on the back doorstep eating, wondering if Bunyan's Celestial City could boast a feast to match this one.

Meanwhile, St. Patrick went about setting up the camera for a new shot. "This has been a busy little stretch for me, Mr. Ax," St. Patrick said as he worked. "That spot you're sitting on was last occupied by another Indian who turned this town upside down."

"What happened?"

"A one-man massacre, that's what. Cherokee Joe himself—

and he rode into town at my side, and me not knowing who he was."

Will Ax was frozen. A biscuit hovered between plate and mouth. "Cherokee Joe? You are sure?"

"Took his portrait myself." He reached into a leather valise on the ground beside the camera stand and pulled out a picture, which he handed to the Indian.

Will Ax stared at the stern black-and-white depiction of Joe Wolfkiller. "Where is this man now?" he asked.

"On the run, unless somebody's caught him. He took off toward the northwest. If he keeps going and fighting like he did here, they may never bring him in—not alive, at least. He fought through a big gunfight that started right where we are now and ended up with him riding out of town like lightning in a saddle. Hah! Since then, I've shot ten, twelve pictures of people back here, near that hole in the wall beside you there. That came from a shotgun blast fired at Cherokee Joe. Folks like to be able to show that they were where something big and bad happened, you know. They love that sort of thing—and it's surely good for my business, I can tell you!"

St. Patrick told the story of Joe Wolfkiller's escape, embellishing it hardly at all, for the true version of the tale was so astonishing, it did not require it. Will Ax continued to eat, but his mind was no longer on his meal. At last he set the tray aside and thanked St. Patrick for his generosity.

"You can thank me by walking right over here and standing . . . yes, right there. Good! Now hold still, tilt your head a bit. Give me that look you did before—no smile, no smile. Look sad and noble. Good, good . . ."

St. Patrick made the photograph and smiled. "That will be a fine one, Mr. Ax. But I want another if you don't mind." He rubbed his chin. "Do you have anything that marks you as a conjurer? Something you could show in the picture?"

Will Ax produced the *ulunsuti*. "This is my divining crystal," he said. "It tells me things I need to know. I thought it had grown useless, but now I believe it just found a new way of talking to me." Before catching himself, Will Ax was about to speculate aloud that the stone, having been bathed in the blood of one white man, had obviously chosen to give its information through the mouth of another white man, St. Patrick.

St. Patrick took another picture of Will Ax, this time with the crystal held before him at chest level. He was so pleased with the view that he decided to take yet another shot. This required him to return to his wagon for a new plate. When St. Patrick returned, Will Ax had gone. He had vanished in a manner appropriately mysterious for an avowed Indian conjurer.

Later, when St. Patrick developed his portraits of Will Ax, he found himself surprised again. The first portrait was excellent, sharp and focused. The second portrait was equally good, except for the middle portion where the *ulunsuti* had been. There, instead of the dull crystal St. Patrick had seen when the plate was exposed, was a brilliant starburst of light, as if the crystal had caught some stray shaft of sunlight and sent it flashing back to the camera fifty times brighter than before. It was a most remarkable phenomenon, even though it did ruin a good photograph.

Will Ax's hunger upon reaching Hutchinson had been minor compared to the agonizing gnawing in the gut of Joe Wolfkiller when he finally reached the town of Great Bend the next day. The town, which stood where the Arkansas River arched down toward the southwest, had broad streets and neat buildings. Joe was weary and empty, and his injured arm throbbed. All the ordeals that he had suffered over the past days were beginning to wear badly on him. He wondered where he could find food.

The day had warmed, but Joe still felt chilled and huddled inside his coat. He hoped the arm was not already infected. Maybe he could locate some whiskey and disinfect it, though he doubted that would do much good after so much time.

Despite the hunger that drove him on, Joe at last realized it was rest or drop. He was at the southwest border of the town. The sky was growing cloudy, and Joe figured it would rain within the hour. The thought of being drenched brought a new chill. He sank down on his haunches and looked despairingly around. A barn stood on the edge of a nearby small farm. Joe rose and wearily made for it. A good sleep in the loft might revitalize him and give his arm a chance to begin healing. He found the barn empty and climbed to the loft. Old heaps of hay were piled all around. He lay down on one heap and pulled more hay up around him. He dozed off, warm externally but still cold inside.

When he woke up, his hunger burned like acid in his gut. He sat up and felt dizzy. His arm was swollen beneath his coat, and he was afraid to look at it. He silently cursed Hambone Coltrane.

Through the open double doors of the barn Joe heard the noise of a door opening and closing at the nearby house. He crept to the wall and peered out through a hexagonal ventilation window. An old woman in a long housedress, apron, and bonnet had come outside and was feeding scraps and bones to a fat dog. The dog ate the scraps quickly and lay down to begin lazily gnawing one of the bones.

Joe watched until the woman reentered the house. He climbed down from the loft and went to the barn door. He peered around it until he was satisfied there was no one to see him. The dog had put its head down to sleep, several bones on the ground beside it. Joe swallowed nervously, then advanced.

Being this hungry, it wasn't hard for him to ignore the indignity of coveting a dog's meal of raw and meaty bones. He advanced through the barnyard, his eyes flickering between the canine and the house, until he reached the picket fence. He lifted his leg and stepped over. The dog stirred, and Joe froze. A few moments later he pulled the other leg over and sneaked right up beside the dog. His hand crept down toward the pile of bones, beef bones with quite a bit of ragged raw meat clinging to them.

The dog sensed Joe's presence and awoke suddenly, leaping up, barking and howling. Joe grabbed a handful of bones and turned to run back toward the fence. He heard the door of the house open as he tried to jump the fence. Any other time it would have been an easy hurdle for him, but today he was so weak that he didn't make it. His boots caught on the pickets and tripped him up. He dropped the bones and caught himself on the ground with both hands, jarring his wounded arm so badly that he groaned. The dog came at him, leaping up and biting at his right boot, which was lodged between two pickets, leaving his foot still inside the fence.

"Don't move!" a tremulous voice ordered. Joe looked back through the fence and saw the old woman on the porch, a shotgun leveled on him. "If you move, I'll have to shoot!" she ordered.

The dog calmed a little now that the woman was there. It backed away and stood with its hackles up, snarling at Joe.

"I want to get up," Joe said.

The woman advanced to the edge of the porch, still holding her shotgun. She was shaking. "You may get up," she said. "But do it slowly."

Joe freed his boot from the fence and stood. He was shaking too, not from fear but weakness and hunger.

"What are you doing creeping around my house?" the old woman asked.

"I was hungry," Joe said. "I came to take the bones you gave the dog."

The old woman blinked. Her expression softened. After a few moments she lowered the shotgun. "You poor man," she said. "Are you that hungry?"

"Yes."

Another pause. "All right, then. Come inside. I'll not send away a man hungry enough to steal the bones from a dog."

Joe thought of running. The old woman came down from the porch, took the dog by its rope collar, and held it. "Come on," she said. "I won't let the dog bother you."

Joe hesitated, then nodded. He climbed over the fence again and walked wearily, dizzily, toward the house.

Chapter 12

Joe Wolfkiller was no philosopher, but he could not help marveling at how peculiar life was. One moment a man can be a renegade on the run, empty, wounded, and the next seated at a table in the homey surroundings of an aging white widow's house, eating roast beef, potatoes, and apple pie from a fancy plate. The old woman, who identified herself as Mrs. Alabama Fleck, widow of the late Stansfield Fleck, Esquire, of Indiana, hovered around the table with a nice little smile, obviously enjoying her task of rescuing the perishing. She kept Joe's coffee cup full and urged plate after plate of food upon him. He refused none of it.

"It's not often I entertain a guest, and never have I had one so obviously in need of a good meal," she said. "I notice, young fellow, that your arm is hurt. Perhaps you should let me call in Dr. Davies and—"

"No!" Joe said a little too sternly. The widow looked a bit taken aback. Joe calmed his tone. "No thank you, I mean. My arm will be fine."

"Whatever you wish, young fellow. Do you mind telling me your name?"

"Henry Feather."

"Feather! Oh, I knew some Feathers back home in Indiana. Gilbert Feather and Audrey—wonderful people. They had the sweetest little baby and named her Downy. Downy Feather—a name that just floats in the air, don't you think? Might you be kin to the Gilbert Feathers, Henry?"

"I don't think so," Joe replied around a mouthful of pie.

"Oh, I guess not. Am I right that you are Indian?"

Joe started to tell her he was only half Indian, then changed his mind. He surely didn't need Alabama Fleck telling people she had given help to a wandering halfbreed, not with the law looking for the halfbreed Cherokee Joe right now. "I'm Cherokee," Joe replied, then wished he had said Choctaw or Creek to steer her even further from the truth.

"Cherokee. Such a lyrical word, *Cherokee*. My son Stanley once had a Cherokee friend. Poor Stanley's gone now, died at Chickamauga during the war. My other son, Jerard, lives in Illinois and has a wife and three children. Then there's my only daughter, Marie, who is in Kentucky at the—"

"May I have some more coffee?"

"Oh yes, oh yes indeed." She bustled to the stove and brought back the pot whose contents Joe had already almost drained.

After she had refilled Joe's cup, Alabama Fleck looked at him seriously and asked, "How did you come to be in so bad a way, Mr. Feather?"

Joe wasn't sure how to answer. He had never been good at coming up with lies off the cuff. "I fell from a train miles up the track," he said, giving her the truth without the details.

"How terrible! I'm sure your companions must be worried about you."

"I was traveling alone."

"I see." She returned the pot to the stove. "Mr. Feather, please don't take offense to this, but your fall from the train left you rather dirty. Let me heat some water for you, and you can bathe in the back room."

"Thank you," Joe said. "That would be good." He sipped his coffee and tried to adjust to the feeling of appreciating a white person. He had somewhat liked Pat St. Patrick, but for Alabama Fleck he was developing a deeper affection. He wasn't used to such gentle cordiality.

The bath was soothing and healing. Joe sat languidly

in the warm water, half dozing. He felt good—or as close to good as he could given his throbbing arm. The wound was beginning to putrify. He washed it gently and bound it with a clean rag he found in a cabinet, then dressed in some oversized clothing Alabama Fleck had left in the room for him while she washed out his clothes. Stansfield Fleck had been a sizable man. When Joe was dressed, he paused by the mirror and used a pair of scissors to clip his hair neatly. Dressed in white man's clothing, groomed and washed, he felt like a completely different person than Cherokee Joe. He hoped he looked completely different too.

When he emerged, his old clothing was drying on a rack near Alabama Fleck's fireplace. She was in the kitchen, putting Joe's dirty dishes into a sink full of soapy water.

"I can't pay you for your help," Joe said.

"Why, I didn't expect you to," she answered. "I'm just trying to give you the kind of help I would want in a time of trouble. Do unto others, you know."

Joe didn't know and didn't ask. "Let me wash those dishes for you," he said.

"Why, thank you, Mr. Feather. You truly are kind."

Joe's arm hurt as he scrubbed the plates. He felt relatively safe here in this house, but inwardly he was still chilled and feeling sick. He hoped his arm wouldn't worsen, for he could not afford to linger here long. There was still the law on his trail, and Caul Slidell to be found.

As he finished the dishes, Joe wondered what to do with Slidell once he found him. It was likely Jim Christmas had learned of Slidell's wrongly reported death by now. If so, Will Ax was probably dead. Joe felt sad. He had come to love that crazy, contradictory old Indian with his big book and divining stone and feet planted in two worlds.

In light of all the uncertainties Joe could think of only one thing to do: Find Slidell and return him to Christmas's house as promised, on the feeble possibility that Will Ax was still alive. If he found Will Ax gone or dead, he would let Christmas experience Cherokee Joe's law of blood firsthand.

Joe had planned to leave Alabama Fleck's house as soon as the dishes were clean. But an offer of a warm bed in a spare room proved impossible to decline. As the evening advanced, Joe felt more and more sick, which he hid from the widow. If he showed his illness, she would fetch that doctor she had talked about, and Joe might wind up identified and jailed.

The next morning, he slept late and ate a big breakfast. The night's rest had done him good, though he was still sick. Only one thing had marred his sleep—the Uktena. Though the dream had made him fearful, in the morning light he found it strangely hope-inspiring. The previous times he had dreamed it, he had been close to Will Ax and his *ulunsuti*. Maybe the fact that he had dreamed it again was an indication that Will was still alive. Joe didn't believe much in such mystical things as portents and dreams, but there seemed nothing wrong with hoping.

Joe was about to leave Alabama Fleck's when a fire in the chimney changed his plans. The old widow had been building up the blaze when a big rush of fire raced up the coated chimney and began gushing smoke back into the room. Joe rushed to the fire with the coffeepot and used the dregs to extinguish the logs. With much effort and at the expense of scorched fingers, he closed the flue and let the fire above burn itself out.

"Thank the good Lord you were here," Alabama Fleck said. "Likely as not, I would have burned the house down otherwise."

"That chimney needs a cleaning," Joe said.

"I know. I've been meaning to do it, but it's hard for me to do, and I hate to impose on others."

Joe nodded. "I'll do it for you," he said. "Then I have to go."

Heights normally didn't bother Joe, but normally he wasn't sick and dizzy as he was today. He climbed up a ladder to the roof with the chimney brush and perched for a long time on the roof peak getting accustomed to the height. A cold wind blasted against him so hard, it threatened to topple him and made him feel sicker. *I'm as crazy as*

Will Ax ever was to be up here, Joe thought. *If I don't break my neck, somebody will see me and fetch the law.*

Nevertheless, he went on with the job. It was actually a pleasure to help Alabama Fleck, who was a full-fledged novelty to Joe Wolfkiller. He had never dreamed people as kind as she really existed; he thought they were nothing but creations of the storybooks forced upon Indian children in the Territory schools, stories designed to make Indians feel they were doing something praiseworthy turning the other cheek every time a hand slapped them. Usually, Joe had noticed, the hand was white.

Up on the widow's roof, Joe had a good view of Great Bend and the plains all around. He looked northward. Somewhere out there, supposedly, was Caul Slidell. How could he hope to find him in so vast a region? The prospect seemed hopeless.

Fighting off a new burst of dizziness, Joe ran the long brush down the chimney again and scraped more black soot off the masonry. He saw something moving down a road that led from the northwest. A wagon, piled with furniture, followed by a carriage. The two vehicles drew closer. At length Joe realized they were approaching an empty two-story house not far from the widow's place.

A white man descended from the loaded wagon when it reached the house and walked back to meet the carriage as it pulled to a stop, a white boy in his teens driving. Its other passengers were two women, one middle-aged and white, the other about Joe's age and obviously Indian. Joe stopped working as she descended. He had never seen so beautiful a young woman.

What was an Indian girl doing with a white family? She was nicely dressed and seemed to be part of the family. He guessed she had been adopted and raised by them, as Will Ax had said his daughter had been.

Then a stunning thought: Could this be Will's daughter? The vehicles had come from the northwest, the direction of Hays City. It was at least possible that this was the very family Will sought. Joe mulled it over, then decided such a thing would be too coincidental.

He watched the women enter the house as the man and boy began unloading the wagon. They were moving into the empty house. Joe waited for the girl to reemerge, but she never did. He finished his work, feeling worse than ever now, and tossed the chimney brush to the ground. His arm hurt badly. He clambered down the roof toward the ladder, and a burst of dizziness washed over him. He needed to get down, fast. The ladder seemed a long way off, though it was only a yard away. Joe reached for it, felt himself waver—and then he fell. The ground rose up to meet him with crushing impact. He groaned, rolled over, and passed out.

When he awoke, he was back in the bed in the widow's spare room. His arm was bound up in new bandages, and he was undressed, buried in covers and propped up on three plush pillows. A white man with mounds of snowy hair was standing beside his bed looking down at him, holding a leather bag like a doctor's valise. Joe swore beneath his breath. Alabama Fleck had gone and done it. She had fetched the blasted doctor.

Joe sat up. "I'm leaving," he said. "Got to leave."

The doctor pushed him back down. Joe was so weak, it was like pushing down a sack of fluff. "You're not going anywhere until you get that arm healed and some strength back, young fellow. If you had let that wound go uncleaned much longer, you'd have lost the arm."

Joe closed his eyes. When he opened them again, the doctor and Alabama Fleck were on the other side of the room talking.

"Just who is he?" the doctor asked.

"His name is Henry Feather. I saw he was sickly when he came, though I didn't know he was this sick."

"An infection will run a man down fast. He's likely gotten worse since he arrived. Tell me, Alabama, you're sure his name is Feather?"

"Well, yes."

"I have a reason for asking. Have you ever heard of an outlaw halfbreed named Wolfkiller? They call him Cherokee Joe most of the time."

"I've heard of him."

"I'm wondering if this man might be one and the same."

Alabama Fleck paused only a moment. "No. I assure you he's not. I've known Henry since he was just a boy. Henry was raised by my dear friends, the Gilbert Feathers of Indiana."

The doctor sounded concerned. "Alabama, you wouldn't be selling me a bill of goods, would you?"

"Dr. Davies, don't you know me by now? You think I'd do that?"

"The answer to both is yes."

"I'm surprised at you."

"You're too good-hearted, Alabama. I don't doubt you'd take in a stray outlaw, just like you took in that stray dog last year."

"Henry would be very upset to be called an outlaw, Dr. Davies. And his family would be scandalized."

"All right, Alabama. I'm taking your word for it . . . but you be careful, hear?"

He gave the widow some instructions on caring for her patient and said he would return the next day to check his progress. When he was gone, Alabama Fleck came to Joe's bedside. "So you were awake?" she asked.

"Yes."

"Then you know why I have to ask you: Are you this Cherokee Joe that Dr. Davies talked about?"

Joe shook his head. "My name is Henry Feather."

She looked at him a long time. Joe wondered if she believed him. Finally she nodded. "If you say you're Henry Feather, you're Henry Feather. That's that."

Joe had a question that couldn't be held back: "Why did you lie to that doctor about knowing me?"

Alabama Fleck pointed toward the wall across from the bed. Joe looked and saw an aging portrait of a stern-looking man with a bald head and fierce eyes. "That was Stansfield Fleck, my late husband," she said. "He was not only a good lawyer but a good man, and not afraid to think and believe differently than those around him. He despised slavery and before the war helped many slaves to freedom at great risk to himself. He also despised the evils done to the Indians of this nation. He was good to every Indian he met, tried to help them, to treat them like they were fellow human beings and not just, well, Indians. You know what I mean."

"I do. Very well."

"Since Stansfield passed on, I've tried to live by the same standard he set. That's why I took you in yesterday and why I lied to Dr. Davies. I want to help you, Henry . . . if Henry you really are."

She left Joe alone and went to begin cooking. He lay in bed staring at the portrait of Stansfield Fleck. He had heard of white men like Fleck, men who really believed an Indian deserved the same rights and privileges of anyone else. Heard of them, but never met one. Too bad the kind was so scarce.

He closed his eyes and slept until Alabama Fleck awakened him for supper, and after that he slept again for the rest of the night.

Chapter 13

J oe was in the most peculiar circumstance of his life. This was no time for him to be laid up in bed, not with the law after him, not with Caul Slidell out there waiting to be found. And that doctor gave Joe the willies with his silence and the suspicious way he looked at him during his calls. Nevertheless, Joe was too weak to ride out just yet, and the truth was he was enjoying the unusual pleasure of a warm bed and a woman who cared for him as lovingly as if he were her own son. Alabama Fleck was giving Joe a new perspective on the white race.

After only two days, Joe's arm was much better, and his illness was substantially gone. The main problem was that the illness had taken his strength. Never before had Joe required so much sleep. Most of his life ha had risen before the sun; now he slept until midmorning. And sleeping away the morning was what Joe was doing when an empty freight wagon rolled into town trailing a small army of boys tossing taunts and occasional stones at the skinny old Indian on the driver's perch.

Alabama Fleck was sweeping her porch when the parade rolled by. Her eyes widened with surprise. Another Indian arriving in Great Bend! First Henry Feather (or whoever he really was) then that pretty adopted daughter of the new family down the street, and now this old white-haired man in a big wagon. It was remarkable.

Will Ax, meanwhile, was having a devil of a time with his young harassers. They were irritating, drew attention to him that he did not want, and were endangering themselves, for just as he was not a very good Methodist or a very good conjurer, he was not a very good wagon driver. He turned onto a side street, nearly running over one boy in the process, and pulled to a stop. As gravel pelted him in the side of the head, he reached into his coat and produced the *ulunsuti* with a great flourish. He raised it above his head, enclosed in his fist. The Remington pistol he had stolen from the wagon's original driver swung menacingly in the gunbelt draped over his shoulder.

"In my hand is a powerful crystal that kills white boys who look on it!" he said. "Leave, or I will open my hand and make you see it!"

The boys, surprised by the old man's dramatic style, backed away. "You're a-lyin'," one said.

Will Ax growled and lifted his fist higher. The boys turned and scrambled away. One tossed a stone back at him and missed by ten feet.

Will Ax grinned and reached toward his pocket to put away the *ulunsuti*. As he did, a ray of sunlight glinted brightly off the stone. The old man examined his crystal. Today it glistened more brightly than it had in a long time. The sight excited him, and he peered into the shining crystal, hoping it could tell him something about Joe Wolfkiller or maybe his daughter.

He received no message from it. He sighed and put away the shining crystal. The *ulunsuti* was still stubborn, still leaving him on his own.

On his own. Well, that would simply have to be good enough. Will Ax looked around at the town. It was all new and strange to him, but at the same time there was something in the atmosphere here that roused a sense of excitement in him, a sense of being close to something or someone of significance. Joe Wolfkiller, maybe. He might be on the next street or around the next corner.

Someone did come around the corner just then. It definitely wasn't Joe. It was a white woman, the tallest and most rotund Will Ax had ever seen. She wore a blue dress the size of a revival tent and carried a blue-barreled shotgun that was almost as long as Will Ax was tall. At her feet were two of the boys who had harassed Will as he came into town. The two were look-alikes, tow-headed and ruddy-cheeked. One pointed up at Will. "That's him, Aunt Pru."

The shotgun leveled down. To Will Ax, the muzzle holes looked as big as twin cannon.

"You threatened my nephews, you foul old coot. Get down from that wagon right now and hand over that gunbelt!"

Will Ax wasn't inclined to disobey. He stood before his rotund captor like a scraggly pine in the shadow of a great oak. Aunt Pru took the gunbelt and handed it to the first boy, who seemed pleased and surprised by the move.

"He pulled something out of his pocket and said it would kill us, Aunt Pru," the second boy said.

"Time for you and me to take a walk, you black-bottomed heathen," the woman said. "I want you to tell the good men down at the jail why you came into our town threatening children."

Will Ax shook his head sadly. Why, he wondered, did the unseen forces that shape a man's destiny determine it was so vital that he meet Aunt Pru today when he had such important things to do? Couldn't this have waited until some more convenient time?

Good questions, but Will Ax expected no answers. There was one good thing balancing the bad: Jails served food—usually good food, and hot.

"I am ready, Aunt Pru," he said, lifting his hands.

They marched off down the street—boys, woman, shotgun, and Indian, making a most interesting processional.

The door opened, and Alabama Fleck came in bearing another trayful of food for Henry Feather. Joe sat up and grinned slightly with closed lips, the closest thing to a full smile he ever gave to anyone. It was obvious that Alabama Fleck was enjoying having someone to dote over; likely she had not been able to do anything like this since her children had left home.

"I hope you like fried chicken," she said. "There's fresh bread and some of those pole beans you enjoy so much. Gravy's in the boat, and there's a good slab of butter to put some flesh onto you. So many of you Indians are just too lean to be healthy. This is the kind of supper you need."

Joe began smearing butter on one of the three thick slices of bread on his tray. No wonder so many white men got fat; Joe was already a few pounds heavier than when he came. As he bit into the bread, Joe wondered if the white men's diet also contributed to their tendency to lose their hair, a characteristic that had intrigued Indians since their first contacts with whites.

"Speaking of lean Indians, you should have seen the old Indian man who rode into town today," said Alabama.

"Old Indian man?"

"Yes." Alabama Fleck was heading over to dust off the portrait of her husband, as she did at least twice daily. She kept her entire house spotless, that portrait the most spotless of all. "He was riding in a big old empty freight wagon and had the whitest hair I've ever seen. He wasn't any bigger around than a telegraph pole. There was the biggest gaggle of boys teasing him all the way into town. Terrible, how boys can be."

Joe was frowning thoughtfully, staring into his coffee cup. Could it be? No... Will Ax was surely still imprisoned or killed by Jim Christmas as useless baggage. "Where did this old man go?" he asked.

"To jail, from what I heard down at the store. Apparently he threatened the boys with some sort of stone. Prudence Flatt hustled him off at the end of a shotgun. Prudence is prone to overdo things when it comes to those foul little nephews of hers."

"Threatened them with a stone..."

"Yes. He would have thrown it at them, I suppose. Humph! I wish he had. They were throwing enough stones of their own at him and calling him indecent names. There's some mothers in this town who could stand to keep a closer eye on their sons, let me tell you. In any case, the poor man is in jail, and everybody is calling him Eagle-eye. He gave his name to the town marshal as Eye of the Eagle or something like that. Henry—you're not eating! Is something wrong with your food?"

"No," he said. "It's good. Very good."

Alabama Fleck smiled. "Eat it all, every bite. You're

looking so much stronger since you've been eating good. I'll be back for the plates later. And in the morning, my best hotcakes, topped with jelly. I'll fatten you up yet, Henry Feather!"

Joe Wolfkiller moved through the dark house on bare feet, making no noise. He carried his boots in his right hand and wore his coat and hat. The gentle snores of Alabama Fleck wafted through the house as he went to her writing desk, took paper and pencil, and in his crude blocky letters wrote her a note of thanks and a promise of repayment for the money he had taken from the little tin cashbox she kept hidden behind a loose stone in her downstairs mantlepiece. Joe had secretly observed her getting money from the box the day before. It made him feel bad to take it, but he could think of no alternative. He had to have some way to buy food and weapons—and maybe to bail out Will Ax if Will Ax it really was down in the local jail. He wished he had been able to steal the widow's shotgun too, but she kept that in the corner of her bedroom, between her bed and the wall. Joe had not felt he could risk waking her by trying to take it.

He felt almost certain that it was Will Ax in that jail. If Will had managed to escape or had been freed for some reason, there was one less worry hanging over him. He could get on with his original quest to kill Caul Slidell and not have to concern himself with Jim Christmas's "bargain" anymore.

One thing Joe tried hard not to think about—the danger of what he was about to do. For Cherokee Joe to walk right into a domicile of the law was quite risky, especially since a broad alert was surely out for him by now. All he had going for him was his chopped-off hair, slightly more filled-out look, and false name of Henry Feather. One thing he was sure he would not have any longer would be the support of Alabama Fleck. She would probably hate him when she discovered he had stolen from her.

Joe left his note and gave a final look around Alabama's house. This place had become familiar and homey to him. Leaving it gave him a sadness strange to one whose feelings seldom broke out of a range bounded on one end by bitterness and on the other by fury.

He left the house and went out to the street. It was a cool, clear night, Great Bend a dark cluster of houses and commercial buildings lining broad dirt streets. Joe walked across town, a moving shadow in the alleys and beneath the eaves. It was as if all the world were asleep except for Joe Wolfkiller. Joe liked the feeling.

At length he found the jail and noted a light burning in the front office. Tight nervousness began to creep up his spine. Someone was in there, awake. He could hear a male voice humming a tune. He walked up to the jail and peered into the window.

A young man sat in a chair tilted against the wall, his feet crossed on the desk. He seemed too young to be a marshal. Joe pegged him as a deputy holding the dull job of tending the jail at night. There was nothing interesting at all about the young man, nothing but the object he was holding up before his face and examining carefully.

The *ulunsuti*. Now Joe knew. It really was Will Ax who was locked away somewhere in there under the name Eagle-eye.

The way Joe saw it, he had two recourses. He could knock, enter politely, and present some of the widow's money to bail out Will Ax. Or he could enter, be not so polite, and take Will out by force. The deputy was just a kid, scrawny and so boyish, he was still freckled. Joe decided to play the situation as it went along. Surely he could get the better of the runty jailer one way or another.

Peering through the window, Joe kept his eye on the deputy as he knocked on the locked door. The young fellow almost fell out of his chair in surprise, obviously not used to night callers. Joe watched through the window as the young jailer put the *ulunsuti* into his pocket, took a small pistol from a desk drawer, and came to the door. He cracked it open a foot and looked out at Joe suspiciously. "What do you want?" For so young a deputy, the voice was deep.

"I've come to bail out the old man you have locked up here."

"Bail out? I don't know that I can do that. Don't rightly know how—that's always been the marshal's job."

"Let me visit him, then."

A long pause. "You an Injun?"

"No."

"You sure do look like one."

"Not me. I hate Injuns. I think the one you got locked up might have stole something from me. Let me in, and I'll see if it's the same one."

"If he stole from you, why do you want him bailed out?"

Joe saw that his lies were crossing each other. To the devil with it, then. He forced the door back, knocking the deputy on his rump. Joe was on him in a moment, wrenching the pistol from his hand. The *ulunsuti* fell from the deputy's pocket and skittered across the floor to the corner. Joe pounded his fist into the deputy's face—once, twice, thrice. The young fellow grunted with the first blow, gasped with the second, passed out with the third. Joe rose and pulled the ring of keys from his belt.

Will Ax was awake, having heard all the ruckus in the office. He rose from his bunk and went to the door, which like the walls and low ceiling of his cell was made of flat bars of iron crossed and bolted together. The door to the office opened, and Will Ax was amazed when Joe Wolfkiller stepped through.

"Hello, old man," Joe said. "Gotten yourself into trouble again, I see."

"Joe, how did..."

"We can talk about it later. I got to get you out of here. I'll have to find which key—"

A fearsome figure suddenly appeared behind Joe, the deputy, hair mussed and face soaked with blood from his nose. In his hands was a sawed-off shotgun, the muzzle of which he thrust against Joe's spine.

Though young, the deputy could cuss almost as impressively as he could revive from a beating. He peppered Joe with every foul name he could muster, which was plenty, then began putting them together in unique combinations. Joe could do nothing but lift his hands and take it, the deputy angry enough that the slightest sign of resistance might prompt him to blast the heart out of Joe's chest.

When the cussing was done, the deputy shoved Joe toward the cell adjacent to Will's. The two cells shared a crossed-bar wall. He forced Joe inside, made him put his hands flat on the wall, and searched him quickly but well. He took the knife from Joe's boot and Alabama Fleck's money from his pocket, then locked him up.

Once Joe was safely caged, the deputy cussed him again for a full minute until his fury was drained. Still bleeding from the nose, he sagged back against the wall. "Don't know who you are, mister, but you'll sure as devil's hell pay for what you done," he said. "Reckon I showed you it ain't smart to pick on this boy, huh?"

He slammed the door behind him and returned to the office. Joe went to the bunk in his cell and sat down onto it, putting his face in his hands. Right now it wouldn't have taken much to make him cry, and he hadn't cried since childhood.

"Cheer up, Joe," Will Ax said. "Everything will be all right."

"You are a fool, old man," Joe muttered.

"No, no—everything really will be all right. I've gotten it back again. See?"

Joe looked up. Will Ax was holding the *ulunsuti* up beside his grinning face. "The deputy kicked it into the cell when he came in. It was a miracle! Pretty wonderful, eh?"

"Yeah," Joe muttered, lying down. His mental eye was inspecting an image of himself on Judge Parker's big gallows. "Wonderful."

Chapter 14

It took Will Ax the rest of the night to dig information out of Joe Wolfkiller, who was far too depressed and angry to want to talk. For the first hour Joe remained mostly silent, softly rubbing his still-healing arm. But by the time the sun was rising, he had told Will what had happened since they parted in the little office room of Jim Christmas's house. Will told his own tale, almost as remarkable as Joe's.

Will Ax was disturbed by Joe's description of the violent encounter at Hutchinson, and forced to face up to the dark and deadly side of his young companion. He wondered if it was right for him to be traveling with, much less giving aid to, so violent a fellow. "Listen to me, Joe," said Will Ax. "This life you live is not a life. It is a road to the grave if you don't get off of it. Death travels the same route you take, and if you do not get off it, you will be overtaken."

"It's too late," Joe said flatly. "I've already killed. I've already run. If the law gets me, it's the noose."

"The law does have you," Will Ax reminded Joe.

"Not for long. I'll find a way out. I'll kill Caul Slidell, and then if I die, I die. It won't matter then."

It required no divining stone for Will Ax to feel the aura of deep, dangerous despair surrounding Joe Wolfkiller. Will weighed his next words carefully. "Joe, maybe you should let Slidell go."

Joe turned on his bunk, staring in disbelief at Will Ax. What Will had said sounded as absurd to Joe as if he had suggested he cut off his own head.

111

"Listen to me, Joe. It is the law of blood you follow that has brought all this evil to you. For every evil thing that comes, you seek to balance it with more evil. That is like trying to empty a bucket by pouring even more water into it, or putting out a fire by fanning its flames brighter. You must learn another way."

"There is no other way."

"There is. It is simply to forget, to put aside. To forgive. I have lived a long time. I have had to forgive many things in my life."

Joe laughed derisively. "You have read too much in your white man's book, Will Ax. It's made you more a fool than ever. The old ways you claim to follow say every wrong must be avenged."

"The world is changing, Joe. Maybe some of the old ways no longer work when the world becomes different."

Joe was surprised to hear that from Will Ax, whom he had perceived as clinging to old ideas and old traditions far more fiercely than anyone else he had known. But he was in no mood for a philosophical discussion today. His biting reply was, "You're not only a poor Methodist and a poor conjurer. You're also a poor Cherokee. You're old and weak. You bend under every wind. Joe Wolfkiller does not bend, ever."

He knew from the look on Will Ax's face that the words had stung. The older man turned away. "Sometimes," he said, "those who will not bend find they can only break."

"I do not break," Joe said haughtily. "I break others."

Will Ax could think only that Joe, locked away in a tiny cell, hardly looked like a man who could break anyone. He felt a wave of fear for the destiny of his violent young companion.

The deputy who brought breakfast to the cells was a big man, at least five inches over six feet with a head the size of a late-summer melon and a look that hinted a melon might be smarter. He wore a dirty yellow shirt with a badge stuck on upside down. He shoved the plates to the prisoners without a word, then stared at Joe for almost a minute. "What's your name, redskin?"

Joe didn't answer. He began gnawing one of the overbaked biscuits from his dirty tin plate.

"You deaf, boy? Answer me!"

"I'm Henry Feather."

"Well, Henry Feather, you've bit off a mouthful of trouble, doing what you did. Is this coot your kin or something?"

"I have nothing to say to you."

"All right, suit yourself. Don't matter to me—I'm just holding down the fort. Henry Feather, huh? I'll sign you in on the book. Herman, he was so tore up last night, he didn't even put your name down. His nose was the size of a baked potato when I come in this morning." The man chuckled.

When he was gone, Joe asked Will Ax if the man was town marshal.

"No, I don't think so. He is a chief of some sort."

"Chief?"

"Yes. Chief Deputy. That is his name. He told me. Town Marshal is gone somewhere, he said, and won't be back for several days."

Joe saw no purpose in pointing out to Will Ax that he was confusing titles and names. He gnawed his biscuit, then devoured the three runny eggs that composed the rest of breakfast. The coffee was so thin, it was like dirty water.

"How long will they keep us locked up?" Will Ax asked. "Chief Deputy told me yesterday that I would probably be free by breakfast."

"It's my fault," Joe replied. "Now that I tried to break you out, they'll probably keep both of us until the marshal gets back."

They talked some more, Will Ax doing most of it. When Will made reference to the daughter he sought, Joe suddenly remembered the arrival of the family with the young Indian lady and told Will Ax of it.

The old Cherokee's face became bright with excitement. "It's her, my little Gatunlati!" he said. "I have felt she was near since I came to this town."

"You don't know it's her," Joe said, but Will Ax didn't

seem to listen. He produced his *ulunsuti* and began looking into it.

"I wish you'd put that rock away," Joe said. "It aggravates me to see you staring into it all the time. What's it saying to you now, old babbler? Does it say when I'll hang?"

"It says only that it wishes you would shut up and quit bothering its keeper so much."

Joe spent the morning waiting for the chief deputy to return and inform him that he had identified him as Cherokee Joe, but that never happened. Joe began to develop a cautious optimism. The chief deputy did not seem a very bright fellow, and with the marshal gone, it was just possible that he would never make the connection between the widely sought Cherokee Joe and the sullen Henry Feather in his cell. Perhaps he would eventually just let his prisoners go. As far as Joe knew, there were yet no official charges lodged against him for the previous night's incident and no talk of courts and judges.

The weather changed as the morning passed. The wind rose, but the day warmed until even the enclosed little cells gave up their chill. The chief deputy opened the office windows and cracked the door to the cellblock, letting the breeze seep in. Will Ax thanked him profusely and told him he was a fine and decent man. Joe could see that Will Ax hoped to flatter his way out of jail.

Joe was dozing later when Will Ax's urgent whisper roused him. "Listen!" said the old man.

Voices caught in midconversation came from the front office. One was the chief deputy's. The other, a smooth talker's, was also familiar, though Joe could not immediately place it.

The chief deputy: "If you're a U.S. marshal, why ain't I heard of you, Mr. Crenshaw?"

"I don't know, Mr. Johnson. But my credentials should speak for themselves."

There was a shuffling of papers. "Well," said the deputy, "it looks square to me. But like I say, you can't talk to Marshal Drenmore because he ain't here."

"That's too bad. Maybe you'll be in a position to help me. You look to be a capable fellow."

"Well, I reckon I do all right."

"Can I give you information that needs to be held in confidence?"

"Why, sure you can!" The chief deputy didn't try to hide his eagerness.

"All right. I'm on special assignment." The voice lowered. "I've been sent to locate and arrest Caul Slidell."

Right then, Joe recognized what Will Ax already had: The deputy's visitor was Jim Christmas.

The chief deputy laughed. "I would have figured you federals would be more up on the news than that. Don't you know that Caul Slidell was gunned down by one of his own men just days ago down about Hutchinson?"

"I know that's the official report, yes."

"Well, then! How you aiming to arrest a man that's already dead, Mr. Crenshaw? You going to dig him up and put chains on him?" The deputy guffawed at his own joke.

"I saw a photograph taken of the body purported to be that of Slidell," said Christmas. "It's the suspicion of my superiors—and my own firm conviction—that the dead man was actually one of Slidell's confederates, named Wiltflower. The two have been mistaken for each other before."

The deputy sounded confused now. "Well, who shot this Wiltflower, then?"

"I don't know yet. Perhaps Slidell himself."

"Why would he do that?"

"For any number of possible reasons. Maybe just an argument. Maybe to lead people to believe, just as they have, that it was Slidell who died. The man had just completed a major robbery at the railroad station in Guthrie, Indian Territory. Old European jewels, purchased by a New York buyer from a wealthy importer in Corpus Christi and in transit by rail by way of San Antonio. It's suspected, on the basis of evidence I cannot divulge at the moment, that Slidell was to divide the jewels with some other coconspirator in the scheme but that he then absconded with all the spoils himself. I believe the shooting of Wiltflower was a deliberate effort by Slidell to throw the law—and perhaps his cheated partner—off his trail by in effect giving the false impression that Slidell was dead."

Christmas had spoken quickly and authoritatively, and seemed to have lost and intimidated the chief deputy, whose answer was a vague "Uh-huh." Joe Wolfkiller was not so dense. Now he understood why Christmas had been so determined to take Slidell alive. Slidell had cheated him, and he wanted the chance to torture the whereabouts of the stolen jewels out of him.

"So, Mr. Johnson, the purpose of my visit here is to ask you if you have any information about the whereabouts of Caul Slidell. You're aware, I'm sure, that the general belief is he is in this county."

"I've heard that, yeah."

"Tell me, then. I'll keep the information in the proper confidence. We certainly don't want average citizens taking out after Slidell and his stolen jewels on their own."

"That ain't likely to happen," the deputy replied. "There ain't nobody around here eager to meet up with Caul Slidell. Folks figure that if he'll leave them alone, they'll leave him alone."

"Does that include the local law?"

"This is just the town marshal's office. As long as Slidell stays out of town, he's not our worry."

Christmas let out a long disdainful sigh through his nostrils. "That's a pitiful attitude for peace officers to have, if I may say so."

The chief deputy took on an offended tone. "We're just doing our job, and that's all."

"I question whether ignoring a murderer and train robber can accurately be called 'doing your job.' But let that lie. Let's put aside our official status a moment. Man to man, can you give me any information, no matter how second- or thirdhand, about Slidell's whereabouts?"

A long pause followed. "I don't know nothing official, but I've heard the marshal say where he thinks Slidell might be. I'll tell you this, Mr. Crenshaw, I don't much like you talking down to me like you have, but since you're federal, I'll help you out. I'll draw you a map. Can't say you'll find Slidell when you get there, but it's where I'd look if I was you."

Joe heard the scratch of a pencil on paper. He looked over at Will Ax and could tell that the old man, as dim as his mental lights seemed to be sometimes, had understood the situation as well as he.

"There you go, Mr. Crenshaw," the deputy said after a few moments. "And good luck to you, especially if you're going after Slidell alone."

"I'm not alone," Christmas said. "See those riders outside? That's my posse."

"It'll take one devil of a posse to get the best of Slidell's hellriders."

"Good day, Mr. Johnson, and thank you for your help."

"So long, Mr. Crenshaw."

The front door opened and closed. Joe and Will Ax heard the deputy give a long low whistle of easing tension.

The door opened again.

"Why, howdy-do, Mrs. Fleck."

Joe and Will Ax exchanged looks of surprise.

"Hello, Mr. Johnson." It was indeed the voice of Alabama Fleck. "I hear you have in custody a young friend of mine. I've come to ask if you'll release him into my care."

"Young friend? You mean the redskin?"

"Unless you've got more than one, I'm sure it's him."

"Fact is, I do have more than one, but only one who's young. The other's old. The young one—says his name's Feather—busted in here last night and gave Herman no end of holy hell—pardon me, holy Hades—trying to bust the old one out. I'm keeping them both penned until Marshall Drenmore gets back."

"Oh, my! Is Herman all right?"

"Busted nose. Looked like a baked potato jammed onto his face when I come in this morning."

"How terrible! I'm surprised Henry would do such a thing."

"Henry . . . yeah, that's his name, all right. Henry Feather."

"Oh, Mr. Johnson, I beg you, please let Henry go. He's an old family friend, and I'm sure he didn't mean any harm. He may have been drinking—the Feather men all have had a certain problem with their liquor, sorry to say."

"Pardon me for saying it, Mrs. Fleck, but this bird sure don't look the type to be no old family friend of somebody like you."

"You can't always judge by appearances, Mr. Johnson. Henry has had a hard life. Please, please let him go in my care. I'll keep him out of trouble."

Joe was amazed by what he was hearing. Why would Alabama Fleck come and plead for mercy for him after he had run out on her hospitality and even taken money from her?

"Well . . . I don't know . . ."

"I'm sure Marshall Drenmore would approve. What charge have you placed against Henry?"

"Ain't really got around to that yet. Waiting on the marshal, you know."

"Oh, dear—the marshal surely won't be happy that you've held an old friend of mine in jail without an official charge!"

The deputy was silent a moment. "You think so?"

"You know Marshal Drenmore—by the book, fair and square. I'm no expert on law, but you do remember, don't you, that the late Mr. Fleck was a licensed attorney? I clearly recall him saying that a jailer can't hold a prisoner without a charge and expect to get away with it. Why, one time he made absolute hay defending a prisoner in a situation like this. The poor jailer lost his job and had to pay a huge fine besides."

Joe grinned. It sounded like Alabama Fleck was pulling a substantial bluff on the dim-witted chief deputy. Why she was doing it was the mystery.

"You telling me straight, Mrs. Fleck?"

"Mr. Johnson! Are you implying I would lie to you?"

"No, no! I'm just thinking, just kind of afraid that . . . Listen, if I turn him over to you and wipe his name off the book here, you think he'd be willing to let bygones be bygones? Shoot-fire, he can even take the old coot with him if he wants. I was half thinking about letting all this go anyway. Ain't no reason to give Marshal Drenmore one more thing to worry about."

Will Ax smiled at Joe. "I think I like this Mrs. Fleck," he whispered.

"I believe Henry will be willing to forgive and forget," Alabama Fleck said. "And certainly I'll say nothing of this. But what about Herman?"

"Herman'll keep his mouth shut if he knows what's good for him," said the deputy. "As far as I'm telling it, he busted his nose going out the door and made up the Injun story to cover up for being clumsy."

Joe heard the rattle of keys and the fast clumping of the deputy's boots on the floor as he headed back to the cells.

"Yes indeed," said Will Ax. "I do believe I like this Mrs. Fleck."

Chapter 15

It was the first time in his life that Joe Wolfkiller had not been able to endure the gaze of another person—and to make it all the more agonizing, this was a woman, a white woman, who had him so humbled. Alabama Fleck's eyes upon him made him feel a shame he had no idea how to handle.

She drove him and Will Ax out of town in her carriage, a fancy rockaway that had been her husband's. She kept the curtains drawn. If it had been anyone but Alabama Fleck, Joe would have figured the curtains were drawn to hide the embarrassment of fraternization with Indians. In Alabama Fleck's case, he knew it was to keep him from being seen for his own sake, not hers. She was still protecting him, as she had before.

Joe wasn't sure why Will Ax had come along. He had opted to leave his commandeered wagon abandoned in Great Bend. Joe did not yet know what his plans were.

Alabama Fleck stopped the rockaway outside town. A horse, wearing an old but good saddle, was tied to the back of the carriage. Joe didn't need to ask for whom it was intended. She was giving it to him. "Henry, I don't know who you are, where you come from, or what you've done, and I don't want to know," she said. "God only knows what it is I see in you and why I feel this need to protect you, but feel it I do."

She turned to Will Ax. "Sir, I don't know you or what

your relationship is to Henry. Nevertheless, I wish you well. I'm sorry I didn't bring you a horse as well, but when I went to the jail, I didn't realize I would be walking out with more than one man. If you're together, you will have to share the horse until you can buy another." She shifted over to Joe again, handing him a leather pouch. "Here. There's money in there, from my bank account. Enough to see you through until you . . . well, until you get wherever it is you're going."

"I have to know why you're doing this," Joe said. He was looking sheepishly at his feet.

"If I knew, I would tell you. I don't fully understand it myself . . . but I think that maybe you're my second chance, my chance to make up for—" her voice broke, and now it was her turn to drop her gaze, "to make up for what my husband did."

"I don't understand."

"I lied to you about Stansfield, Henry. I told you he was a man of open mind and sympathy for Indians. He wasn't. Years ago, back in Indiana, Stansfield allowed a young Indian man to be lynched for horse theft. The poor man was innocent. It was Stansfield's nephew by his first marriage who had stolen the horse, and Stansfield knew it. He steered the vigilantes in the wrong direction, told them it was the Indian, our own stableman, who did it. Stansfield carried the guilt of that to his grave. Maybe it's what finally killed him. I never knew of it until the hour before he died. He confessed it to me, poured it out on me like scalding water. I still can feel the burn of it. . . ." She shuddered. "I vowed that day that if ever I had the opportunity to help someone like that poor stableman, so help me, I would do it. I remember that sad young man's face so clearly—sometimes see it in my sleep. He was much like you, Henry."

She paused, wiping away her tears on a silk handkerchief she dug out of her cuff. "I don't know that what I've done is right. I've lied to the law. I've set free a man who may be guilty of things that would horrify me. I don't know, and I don't want you to tell me. All I want to remember is that I gave a second chance to a young Indian named Henry Feather. Whatever you might have done,

Henry, whoever you might really be, I hope you will take this chance I've given you and make good with it. You've seen many bad things in your life—I can see it in your eyes. I want the satisfaction of knowing that I've let you see at least one good thing." She leaned forward and kissed Joe's cheek. "Goodbye, Henry Feather. God go with you. If I've done wrong today, may God forgive me."

She turned away and went back to the carriage. Will Ax had already freed the horse and was holding its reins. He and Joe watched as Alabama Fleck climbed into the seat and drove away.

For a minute or so the two men remained silent, alone on the flatlands outside town.

"She was right, Joe. It is best she doesn't know who you are and what you've done," said Will Ax. "I wish I myself didn't know what you've done."

Joe wheeled to face him. "Are you my judge now, old man? If you think I'm so bad a man, why don't you just get away from me?"

"I've been asking myself that question. I think maybe it's because you need somebody to take care of you. Besides, it was you who came to me in the jail, not me to you."

"Yes, but you came to Great Bend to find me. You didn't have to do that."

"Yes I did. I couldn't let you ride under Caul Slidell's gun still thinking I was a prisoner of Jim Christmas. I couldn't have you shot down trying to protect me when I no longer needed protection."

Joe looked back toward town, watching Alabama Fleck's rockaway disappear.

"What will you do now?" Will Ax asked.

"What I planned from the beginning. I'll go and avenge my father by killing Caul Slidell. Now I'll have to find him before Jim Christmas does."

Will Ax nodded sadly. "That's what I thought you would say."

"And what about you?" Joe asked.

"I'm going back to town. I'm going to find this Indian girl and see if she is my little Gatunlati."

"And if she isn't?"

"She will be."

"The *ulunsuti* has told you, eh?"

"No. This time it's just me who tells me. I can feel that Gatunlati is close. Soon I'll have given her my treasure and can go on to the Celestial City in peace."

"You talk like you want to die, Will Ax."

"No, Joe Wolfkiller, it's you who wants to die. Else you wouldn't do the things you do."

Parting with Will Ax was more difficult for Joe than he had anticipated. With Will Ax perched behind him on Alabama Fleck's horse, he rode back as close to town as he felt he safely could. His heart was heavy, which he found inexplicable. He should be happy. He was free, had escaped identification in the jail, and had a horse, courtesy of Alabama Fleck. Furthermore, Will Ax had given him the Remington pistol he had taken from the original driver of Jim Christmas's freight wagon. The weapon had been returned to Will when he was freed from jail. Now Joe could continue his quest for Caul Slidell unimpeded.

The strange thing was, he wasn't sure he wanted to. Joe was growing weary of this violent journey. He had killed men and found no glory in the killing. It was the strangest thing. He didn't want to be Cherokee Joe anymore. He wanted only to be Joe Wolfkiller, unknown, unsought, living the quiet life of a normal man. Too late for that. He had already set his course. He could not undo what had been done.

Will Ax climbed down from the saddle and stood looking up at Joe. There were tears in his eyes as the wind stirred his stiff white hair. He looked very small and frail. He reached inside his coat and pulled out his leather-bound book. Handing it up, he said, "For you. I am finished with it now."

Joe reached down and took the volume. He started to say something but could not find his voice, so he merely nodded.

"Maybe we will see each other again, Joe, if ever you can find your way out of the City of Destruction. If we don't, I'm glad to have ridden with you."

Joe cleared away the knot in his throat. He slipped the book into his coat pocket. "I hope you find your daughter, old man."

"I'll find her," said Will Ax. "Very soon now I'll be with her."

Joe watched him walk away toward Great Bend, then turned the horse and rode slowly away.

It was night, but the wind still blew warm across the flatlands. Will Ax stood beneath a squatty tree and stared across the street at a tall house that spilled light from its big windows. This was the house that Joe had described to him, the house where the Indian girl lived.

The old man's heart was beating fast. Now that he felt so close to the end of his quest, he found he was not nearly as courageous as he had thought he would be. How could he approach a young lady who had never known him and tell her he just might be her true father? And how could he prove that he was, even to himself, much less to her?

No answers to those questions appeared. Will Ax scratched his chin, shuffled his feet, and felt more nervous than ever. Another walk was what he needed. Another slow trek through Great Bend to calm his nerves.

A shadow passed across an upper window in the house. A curtain pulled to the side, and a young woman looked out. She was silhouetted in the light, so Will Ax could not see her features, but he knew it was she. "Gatunlati," he whispered. "My baby girl." The girl moved away from the window, and he saw her no more.

Yes, another walk was definitely in order. He began trekking along slowly, his hands deep in his pockets, his white hair wisping out on both sides. A couple of men rode by, and one of them spat a dollop of tobacco juice toward him, barely missing. The men laughed coarsely and made a comment about "lousy redskins, dirtying the streets," then passed on by. Will Ax paid them no heed.

As he passed a livery stable, the big door swung open. Will looked inside and saw the commandeered freight wagon he had abandoned. Beside it stood Jim

Christmas, Miller, and a gaggle of others. Will's eyes
swept to the man who had opened the door. It was the
wagon driver he had pounded senseless out on the road
north of Wichita. The old Indian backstepped into a dark
alley. He could hear Christmas's voice.

"That's the wagon, sure enough," Christmas said.
"Reckon that old redskin drove it all the way here?"

"Sure appears so," another man said. "Or maybe
somebody took it from him. It was sitting parked on the
street when we found it."

The wagon driver returned to Christmas's side. Christmas looked at him with displeasure. "I can't believe you
let that skinny old heathen steal my wagon."

"I told you how that happened, Jim. I swear it must
have been an anvil he hit me with."

"Hell, forget it. What's done is done. Come on—let's
all go find us a little relaxation," said Christmas.

Will Ax watched them stride out of the livery and to
the left, relieved they had not seen him but glad he had
seen them, for it reminded him that he had to be careful
as long as Christmas remained in town. He hoped Joe
would not encounter Christmas during his quest for Slidell.
Christmas would certainly kill Joe if he had the opportunity.

Will continued his walk but made sure he stayed in
the darkest areas. His thoughts returned to the big house
and the girl inside it. Part of him felt ready to return and
knock on the door, but a bigger part of him was still too
scared. He kept walking until finally he had circled back
near the house again. Then he stood as before, looking up
at the bright windows.

"Well, old man—you going in or not?"

The voice came from behind. Will Ax wheeled. His
eyes widened as Joe Wolfkiller stepped forward. "Joe—
you have killed Slidell already?"

"No. I still have that ahead of me. I thought about my
quest after I left you today . . . and I thought about yours.
Yours seemed more important. So I came back." Joe
nodded toward the house. "She's in there."

"I know. I saw her at the window."

"Then why haven't you gone to meet her?"

Will Ax looked sheepish, then put on a smile. "I'll go,

soon. But first let's celebrate your return, Joe. Let me take you to a saloon."

"I can't risk going into a saloon."

"Oh . . . you're right. I can, though."

"Lead the way, old man."

Together they walked toward a well-lighted tavern on the far side of town. Joe was glad he had come back to Will Ax, though coming back made little sense. Sensible or not, he wanted to know if the girl in the house really was Will's daughter, wanted to see the old man's happiness at reuniting with her if she was. Joe's was a quest of death, Will's a quest of life that roused in Joe an aching longing for something that he could not explain or identify. Ironically, Joe Wolfkiller, the halfbreed who had so long been enamored of living on the edge of death, was now becoming enamored of life.

Outside the tavern Joe gave Will Ax money and drew back into the alley beside it to await his return. As he waited, he fiddled with the Remington pistol, adjusting to the feel of it and wishing he also had a good rifle or shotgun. A handgun had too many limitations. Maybe in the morning he could get Will Ax to buy a rifle for him as he was buying the bottle right now.

Time passed, and still Will Ax did not return. Joe turned the Remington's cylinder, listening to the clicking whir of the oiled mechanism. He unloaded the pistol and took a few practice pulls on the trigger, determining its action and sensitivity. He reloaded the pistol and holstered it. Still no Will.

Growing impatient, Joe walked around the back of the saloon and over to the far side. There was a window there, wide and hinged on the top so it could be left open in the rain. Closed tonight, it provided a clear view into the saloon. The window was located behind the long bar and gave Joe an angle of view roughly equivalent to the barkeep's. What it showed him was startling.

Will Ax was being held against the bar by Jim Christmas. Christmas had a big cruel grin on his face as he pushed the tip of a knife against Will Ax's throat. His men stood around, laughing and enjoying the treat of seeing their superior terrorize the Indian who had escaped him and stolen his wagon. Others in the saloon were also enjoying the show. Two or three seemed disturbed by it, but no one was lifting a hand to stop it.

Joe's fury roused like a sleeping lion and roared. Jim Christmas would not get away with this. Joe was just about to head around the front door when Christmas pulled out his pistol and whipped Will Ax hard across the side of the face. Will Ax slid down. He would have collapsed completely had he not been wedged between Christmas and the bar.

That did it. Joe's anger flared beyond his control. He backed up and ran toward the window, thinking as he leaped that Christmas was about to get the surprise of his life. The leap was made with the instinctive grace of a cat springing upon a bird. Joe's uplifted knees shattered the window and his entire body launched through, landing him directly behind the bar. One spring, and he was atop it.

Will Ax, badly stunned by Christmas's blow, looked up. "Joe..."

Christmas, meanwhile, had staggered back, his eyes big. Will Ax slid to the floor. Christmas's men fell back, too amazed to react to the fearsome halfbreed with anything more than stares.

Christmas looked into Joe's eyes and saw a dead glitter in them that made him winter-cold to the soul. "Cherokee Joe!" he said with awe and alarm. "That's Cherokee Joe!"

Then Christmas reached under his jacket for the pocket pistol he kept hidden there. He hardly had it cleared when Joe's Remington spoke. The first bullet struck Christmas in his ribs, driving him back.

Grunting, he hunched down and fired a random shot that passed into the floor. Christmas's men, loyal only to his dollars, backed away and gave no assistance. Christmas swore, lurched forward, and lifted his pistol again.

This time Joe shot him through the heart. As he died, Jim Christmas fired one final blast, the jolt of the shot flipping the pistol from his weakening hand. The slug missed Joe by several feet.

It did not miss Will Ax. The old Indian had pushed

himself up at the wrong moment, and the slug caught him in the side.

Joe yelled, "No!" He leaped down from the bar and came to Will Ax's side.

"Joe . . . he's killed me, Joe."

Tears in his eyes, Joe scooped up the crumpled form of his friend and carried him out the front door. Joe's horse was tethered nearby, and he heaved Will Ax onto it, then slid into the saddle, gave a yell, and rode off, no one daring to stop him.

Chapter 16

Rebecca Pullette darted across the street just in time to avoid being knocked down by three riders who galloped too fast around the corner. The pretty young Cherokee lady paused beneath a windmill well pump and collected herself before continuing on toward her house. That had been close. She had not even heard them coming. Her heart thumped in excitement over the near accident.

She wondered who the riders were. They wore big hats and long coats, and there were about a dozen others just like them in town. They had arrived by train the day before on a special car with closed shades, their horses riding in locked boxcars. Folks who had watched the special train unload talked about the several crates of rifles and ammunition that composed the only cargo besides men and horses.

All Rebecca knew about the mysterious newcomers was that they were federal men who had come for some reason having to do with the railroad. Rebecca did not know what the reason was; young women were seldom told of such masculine matters and in the Pullette house were expected not to ask.

Keeping a more careful eye now, Rebecca continued down the street and around another corner. From here she could see her house, the big impressive place that seemed like a palace to her in comparison with the much smaller house the Pullettes had occupied in Hays City. Ross Pullette, Rebecca's adoptive father, had worked hard during the early lean times in Hays City, and it had paid off. Through overfrugal living he had managed to save enough to buy into a promising hardware and feed business here in Great Bend, and through some additional dealing and bargaining had obtained their new house at an excellent price. The move to Great Bend just a few days back had been a time of joy for all the Pullettes.

Yet for Rebecca a vague and ominous feeling had accompanied the joy. Since Great Bend came into her view as she rode in on the carriage seat, she had felt tense, expecting the unexpected. Her feelings mystified her, and she tried to explain them away as simple nerves, but that was not convincing. That first sight of Great Bend filled her with the conviction that something was coming her way, something significant and unusual.

Already half of that expectation had been fulfilled. Plenty of unusual things had come along in her brief time in Great Bend. First there was the sight of that slender young Indian chimney sweep atop a nearby house the day the Pullettes moved into their own. Why he struck her as unusual Rebecca had not yet figured out. Then there was that second Indian, the old man who stood across the street in the darkness watching her window. He had frightened her and also intrigued her.

Unusual things had come not only to Rebecca but to all of the town. First there was that terrible gunfight at the tavern. According to what she had overheard, it had involved a young halfbreed outlaw people called Cherokee Joe and a stranger who had come to town claiming to be a federal marshal but now was thought to be a powerful Wichita businessman named Christmas. According to what Ross Pullette had said at last night's dinner table, the law was trying to finalize his identification even now. Whoever he was, he was thoroughly dead, and before he had been gunned down, he had publicly called his assailant Cherokee Joe.

Then, as if all that wasn't enough, the posse of riders had showed up on the train and had been galloping hell-for-leather all around town ever since, flashing rifles and pistols and stirring a crazy quilt of contradictory rumors, most of them tied to Cherokee Joe. Rebecca had heard several theories about them so far but had no idea which if any was true.

As she continued into her yard, she glanced at the house where she had seen the Indian chimney sweep that first day. Could he have been Cherokee Joe? That possibility had suggested itself as soon as she heard of the fatal shooting in the tavern. And that old man outside her house—might he have been the old Indian who reportedly was being protected by Cherokee Joe in that gunfight? Rebecca wondered, thinking she would never answer those questions.

She found out more at that night's supper table. Ross Pullette was in an unusually talkative mood. He had been in town all day and had picked up the latest information about the Cherokee Joe incident, the man who had been shot, and the riders who now circulated throughout the town.

"Despite what you might have heard, those riders didn't come to Great Bend looking for this Cherokee Joe fellow," he said. "I've got good information. They're a specially formed federal posse come to find and capture Caul Slidell, the outlaw. You've all heard of him, surely. This Slidell pulled off a robbery at a train station down in the Indian Nations and came riding up this way. Supposedly he hides out in this county from time to time. Well, the railroad was plenty riled about the robbery, which involved the murder of some Indians, sorry to say. The railroad barons pulled all their strings in Washington to get something done about Slidell. Next thing you know, there's a federal posse put together. That's who those riders are."

"So why are they still in town?" asked Jimmy Pullette, Rebecca's adoptive younger brother.

"Complications, from what I hear. It seems this fellow Cherokee Joe shot down was named Jim Christmas. I've heard of him—wealthy and powerful gent down about Wichita. Had ties to the railroad. And listen to this: There's federal suspicion that he was backing Slidell in that train-station robbery and that Slidell cheated him out of his share of the loot. Furthermore, one of the Indians who was killed during the robbery was Cherokee Joe's father. Amazing, huh? All these things are fitting together, and the federal marshals leading the posse are trying to make sense of it all. Add to that a rumor that the local law actually had Cherokee Joe in jail before the shooting and then turned him loose without identifying him, and you can see how confusing it all gets. It's really slowed up that posse. Funny part is, the local deputy who supposedly turned Cherokee Joe loose is trying to weasel out by blaming the whole thing on that old widow up the street." Ross Pullette chuckled.

"The one in the big house you can see from the yard?" Rebecca asked.

"That's the one."

"Oh!" She took another bite as she mulled the realization that it was at that very house she had seen the Indian chimney sweep. Now it seemed even more likely it had been Cherokee Joe.

"Seems to me the posse ought to go after Cherokee Joe before they worry about Slidell," Jimmy Pullette commented. "I was told today that he's killed peace officers in the Indian Territory and down in Hutchinson too."

"So he has," Ross Pullette replied. "But I doubt this posse will concentrate much on Cherokee Joe. The only reason it officially exists is to deal with Slidell. The railroad cares a lot more about him than some short-lived triggerman like Cherokee Joe."

"Short-lived? You mean he's dead?" Rebecca's adoptive mother asked.

"Not yet," Ross Pullette replied around a mouthful of beef. "But he will be. Men like that don't live long. Like my father always said, 'If a bullet doesn't lay a bad man low, a noose will lift him high.'"

"If he killed that man because he was tormenting an old Indian, then maybe Cherokee Joe isn't so bad," Rebecca said.

"Rebecca!" her mother responded. "How can you talk so? He's a killer! A murderer!"

Rebecca flushed. "I'm sorry," she muttered. "It was just a thought."

"And hardly a good one," her mother muttered.

"Let it go, Mother," Ross Pullette said. "Pass those potatoes, will you?"

Rebecca said nothing more during the rest of the meal. Her ears burned in embarrassment at the comment she had made. She had surprised herself as much as her mother by her sentiment. She didn't mean it, not really. Cherokee Joe surely was very bad if he really had killed men of the law. Still, the story she had heard was that no one else had stepped in to help the poor old Indian being tormented by that Christmas fellow. If Cherokee Joe was bad, at least he was also willing to protect the downtrodden.

Rebecca finished her meal, said she didn't feel well, and excused herself to her bedroom to turn in early. Once beneath her covers, she found she could not sleep. She kept thinking about all the excitement in town, about all the talk and drama, about Cherokee Joe and the old man he had protected.

The clock ticked on the wall. Outside, horsemen passed, the restless posse members sweeping through town again. When they were gone, there came a lull, and the howling of a dog somewhere outside town sounded lonely and a little scary. Rebecca Pullette pulled up the covers, shivered, and went to sleep.

She awoke without knowing why, staring up toward the high ceiling. Sleep had been fitful all night. She had dreamed about Cherokee Joe, seeing him in the form of that Indian chimney sweep atop the widow's house. When she sat up now, she thought she was dreaming still.

Silhouetted in her window, which gave onto the roof of the porch, was the form of a man, a slender man, and young, clad in a long coat, denim pants, and a flat-brimmed hat. Rebecca Pullette drew back in fear. The window behind the man was open, the curtains blowing in the breeze that stirred through. He had come in across the porch roof.

"Don't be afraid," he said in a whisper. "You have nothing to fear from me."

"Who are you?"

"That isn't important. I've come to take you to your father."

"My father is downstairs. If he finds you here, he'll shoot you."

"It's your real father I mean. Your Indian father."

Rebecca drew in her breath. Her Indian father! She had no memory of the man, knew nothing about him except what little her adoptive parents had told her. She had often wondered if he still lived, and what he was like.

"My real father . . ."

"Yes. Or so he is convinced. His name is Will Ax."

Rebecca knew she should scream, but she didn't. What she was hearing was too intriguing. Fascination was beginning to overwhelm fear, and this despite her rising suspicion that the young intruder was Cherokee Joe himself and the old man he was calling her father was the same one he had protected in the tavern.

"But how can I know what you're saying is true?" she asked.

"You can't. But you've got to believe it is, like Will Ax does. Come on. There isn't much time, and it's not safe for me here. Don't be afraid of me. I promise you on the blood of our fathers that I'll let no harm come to you."

"Are you Cherokee Joe?"

A pause. "That's what the white men call me. My name is Joe Wolfkiller."

Rebecca looked around the room. It was the room of an American white girl, domestic, familiar, tame. The dark figure of Cherokee Joe was out of place here . . . and suddenly, she felt out of place too. The wind blowing in through the window, the slender man before her, the prospect of a meeting with a father she could not remember— these things awakened a deep wild impulse in her. She could not remain in this house tonight. Tonight she belonged out there on the open land with Cherokee Joe. This was what that sense of something significant coming her way was all about. The feeling was overwhelming now, but not ominous as before.

"I'll come with you," she said. She rose, her nightgown like a white shroud around her, and went to her wardrobe for her clothing.

Cherokee Joe turned away as she dressed, looking out

the window in a posture as tense and fragile as a catgut string. "He is badly wounded," Joe said. "He was shot."

"Will he live?"

Joe answered only after a pause. "No. I don't believe he will." Rebecca watched him lift his hand and touch his face, still turned away from her, and realized with surprise that the feared outlaw Cherokee Joe had just wiped away a tear. "I wanted to find him a doctor, but he wouldn't let me leave him. Now it is too late for doctors."

Ten minutes later, Rebecca Pullette was riding behind Joe Wolfkiller, feeling a great sense of unreality. As they rode, he told her more fully the story of Will Ax and his quest.

Rebecca's arms were around Cherokee Joe's waist, and her cheek rested against the back of his shoulder. The wind whipped her hair. She knew she was foolish for being here. It did not matter. She had done what she wanted to do, and this would be a night she would not forget for the rest of her life.

Will Ax's eyes blinked as warm drops fell upon his face. He looked up at the crude leaky roof of boards above him and hoped the rain would not be so heavy that water would fill the little gully in which he was lying. A gully was no place for a wounded man to rest, but he did not fault Joe Wolfkiller for placing him here. There was no other good place to hide on the flatlands.

It was terribly dark. Will Ax felt alone.

The boards that so poorly sheltered him had been put in place by Joe Wolfkiller, who had found them scattered about the ruin of an old shack foundation nearby. Joe had built the crude ground-level shelter over the gully and then tended Will's wound as best he could. Upon seeing the bloody hole, Joe had looked grim and declared that he would return to Great Bend for the doctor. No, Will had told him. If you return, you'll die, and I'll be left out here alone. I don't want to be left alone. If you stay with me, I will live. The *ulunsuti* has told me.

So Joe had stayed, and Will had waited for his miraculous healing. It had not come, and now Will knew it would not. He was too sick to get better, no matter what the *ulunsuti* said. He was going to die. The thought bothered him some, though not as much as the feeling of aloneness overwhelming him now. "Joe?" He said the name as loudly as he could and was surprised to find his voice nothing more than a weak, grating whisper. "Where are you, Joe?"

No answer came. Joe had abandoned him. Will closed his eyes, and tears mixed with the rain on his face. He had not thought Joe would leave him to die alone.

A suspicion came, making Will open his eyes again. Might Joe have gone back to Great Bend to get a doctor, despite Will's urging to the contrary? He hoped not. No doctor would come with an outlaw killer onto the plains in the middle of the night just to tend a dying old Indian. Joe would only be endangering himself needlessly.

The rain passed over, and no more drops fell on Will's face. He dug his hand into his pocket, held the *ulunsuti* in his fist, and slept again. When he awakened, he no longer felt alone. Yellow light flickered on the underside of the low board shelter. Will was confused.

"Old man, I see you're still alive," a familiar voice said from the end of the shelter.

"Joe . . . I thought you had left me."

"Only for a while. I had to go fetch someone to you."

"If you've brought a doctor, it's too late. Death is in my heart, Joe."

"Tell it to wait long enough for you to meet who I brought."

Joe Wolfkiller lifted the boards above Will Ax and laid them aside. The old man watched Joe, too weak to lift his head, and wondered whom he had brought and why he felt such a mounting excitement. Then before him was a face, feminine and dark, beautiful in the flickering light of the little fire Joe had built farther down the gully, the first fire he had dared to make since fleeing Great Bend.

"Gatunlati?"

Rebecca Pullette smiled and knelt beside the old man. "Yes, Father. I've come to you."

"Gatunlati!" said Will Ax, and as weak as he was, he managed to lift his arms and put them around Rebecca. She lowered herself to let him hold her.

For several minutes after that they talked. Joe stood off to the side by the fire, watching, his slender form dangerously exposed. He did not care. The only thing that seemed worth caring about at the moment was happening a few yards away where Will Ax was at last fulfilling his final quest.

Rebecca Pullette watched silently as Joe Wolfkiller pulled Will Ax's old Union coat up over the old man's unmoving chest, upon which now lay the Bunyan volume, and then over his face.

Joe patted the dead man's shoulder, stood, and looked at Rebecca. His eyes were red and damp, and this time he did not try to hide his emotions. "Thank you," Joe said. "You made him happy in his last hour."

"He said strange things at the end," Rebecca said. "He spoke one moment of joining the spirits of his fathers and the next of crossing a river and going to some great city, and of Jesus and the cross. He talked like..."

"Like a man living in two worlds," Joe replied. "That's the way Will Ax lived, and it's the way he died."

"He really believed I am his daughter," Rebecca said.

"Maybe you are."

"No. I know very little about my father, but one thing I do know—he had only one arm. He lost the other during a battle in the big war."

Joe nodded, thinking it would have been better not to know what Rebecca had just told him. "I suppose it doesn't matter. To him, you were Gatunlati. You were real."

"He gave me this... he called it his treasure." Rebecca held up the *ulunsuti*.

The sun was rising over the horizon, and some of its light struck the crystal. Joe was surprised to see that it did not cast back the light as it had other times he had seen it. It was dark and dead. Its light had faded with the life of its keeper.

"I don't understand what it is," Rebecca said.

"Once it was an *ulunsuti*, the most powerful of the Cherokee divining crystals," Joe replied. "Now I think it is just a stone like any other." He looked down at the still body at his feet. "Or maybe it was always just a stone. Maybe it just reflected the spirit of Will Ax, like its surface reflected the sun. I don't know much about such things."

Rebecca held the *ulunsuti* close to her, cupping it in her hands. "I will always treasure it," she said.

"Yes. You should," Joe said. "Now we have to ride. I'll take you as close to town as I can safely go. It's time for you to go home."

Chapter 17

J oe, weary and dirty, sat beside the newly covered grave he had scraped out with a board and filled with the body of Will Ax. The effort might have been wasted, for the grave was shallow and could easily be dug up by burrowing animals. Nevertheless, the burial seemed important to Joe. He could not let his friend's corpse lie on the open plains like that of some dead dog.

Deep loneliness settled over Joe as he sat looking at the grave. Not until now did he realize how much he had come to love Will Ax. He hoped Will had found his way to the Celestial City he talked about so much.

He stood and stretched his tired muscles. On the ground nearby lay a rabbit he had snared. Joe scrounged around in the scrubby brush for fuel to roast a late breakfast. As he skinned the rabbit and roasted it on a stick, Joe thought about Rebecca Pullette. On the way back to Great Bend he had asked her why she had come with him to see Will Ax when a single question—whether Will had one arm or two—would have let her know he was not really her father.

Rebecca had not given a very clear answer. It came to this: She had come because she had wanted to. Because it seemed right. Because, despite her raising, she remained Cherokee in heart and heritage. Whether Joe could understand that she did not know.

"I do understand," Joe replied.

Rebecca told him of events in town since the shooting, including the arrival of the posse searching for Caul

Slidell. Joe asked when they would ride out, but Rebecca didn't know.

He left her within walking distance of Great Bend. She would find trouble at home, she speculated aloud, for by now surely they knew she was missing. She didn't care. She was glad she had met Will Ax, glad she had met Cherokee Joe.

Joe watched her walk away and thought how it might have been had he known her under other circumstances—if he had been simply Joe Wolfkiller and not Cherokee Joe, outlaw.

The rabbit was hardly enough to fill Joe's empty stomach, but it would have to suffice. He stood, wiped his hands, and went to Will's grave a final time. He looked down upon it thoughtfully, reached into his coat pocket, and pulled out Will's leather-bound book.

"You may as well keep it, old man," he said. "I doubt I'll find any bright cities at the end of my road." He tossed the volume onto the grave, mounted, and rode away.

An hour later he halted at the base of a low slope. On the other side he heard the noise of many horses. Dismounting, he slipped to the top and peered over. A band of horsemen in long coats were riding north. Their route indicated they had come from Great Bend.

This had to be the posse Rebecca had told him about, setting off at last to find Caul Slidell. Caul Slidell—the killer of Joe's father, the man Joe had vowed to kill.

Joe went back to his horse, mounted, and after several minutes rode to the top of the rise. The horsemen were faint specks in the distance. Joe watched them until they were nearly out of sight, then turned his mount to ride in the opposite direction. He got only a few yards before he turned again and eyed the receding riders. Swearing at himself, Joe fell in behind, following their trail.

The cluster of buildings where Caul Slidell and his hellriders made their occasional camp had once been a ranch, but had been abandoned four years ago. Its former occupants could hardly have imagined that their spread would become the scene of the sort of violence taking place today.

Caul Slidell, bleeding from a shallow leg wound, grimaced and bobbed up to send another slug from his Winchester speeding toward the hiding place of one of the long-coated gunmen who had descended upon the hideout an hour before. Slidell was inside what had once been a stable, fighting out of the loft along with three of his hellriders. Within Slidell's view three other hellriders lay dead in the clearings between buildings. So far, he had seen only one of the attackers killed. His men, badly surprised by the assault, were taking the worst of it.

Who were these long-coated gunmen? Some sort of lawmen maybe, or perhaps private guns hired by the railroad—or by Jim Christmas, curse his soul. Whoever they were, they were the first to take on Caul Slidell's hellriders in their home base. No one, law or otherwise, had dared try anything like this before.

Slidell lifted his rifle and took another shot at one of the gunmen. He missed. Swearing, he levered in another bullet. Yeah, it was Jim Christmas behind this, sure as the devil. Jim Christmas, mad because Slidell had gotten the best of him.

Maybe it had been a mistake to cheat Jim Christmas out of his cut of the stolen jewels. Maybe the mistake had been to deal with Christmas in the first place. Slidell had had a gut feeling it would turn bad. The whole thing had taken on a sour taste ever since he had shot down Ed Wiltflower back around Hutchinson.

Still, he couldn't regret it all. The haul at the Guthrie train station had been the richest of his career. Already he had used a contact, set up, ironically, by Jim Christmas, to convert the jewels to cash before Christmas could get word out to abort the transaction. Part of the cash Slidell had divided among his hellriders. His own cut, the largest, was safely stashed where only he could find it. He had been only an hour from going to fetch it and disappear for a few months when the attack had come.

One of the attackers darted across a clearing, hurdling

one of the dead bodies. Slidell fired another ineffective shot. The gunman dropped and rolled, coming up behind the stone wall of a well, raising his rifle and firing. One of the men fighting beside Slidell jerked and pitched backward, blood pooling around him. The slug had entered his skull and killed him instantly.

"We can't whip 'em, Caul!" one of his remaining gunmen declared. "Them fellows, they're trained fighters—you can tell. I seen a federal badge on one of 'em. We'll have to give it up."

Slidell barked an order to keep shooting, then headed around to the other side of the loft. Peering out, he saw nothing encouraging on the other side. Two more dead men, both hellriders, and another, seemingly wounded. Slidell swore.

Behind him, the gunman who had talked surrender yelled and fell back, a bullet through the chest. He died looking accusingly at Slidell.

The outlaw swore again, stood, and leaped out of the loft. Pausing at the door of the barn, he fired another shot at one of the attackers and was gratified to see the man fall. He didn't get up. Slidell took a quick look around, drew in a breath, and ran across the clearing toward an adjacent building.

He drew no fire. Apparently no one had noticed his flight. Inside the building he paused to reload his Winchester with the last of the cartridges in his pocket. He was beginning to see that the hellrider in the loft had been right: This was one battle he and his men could not win. Used to law that turned its eyes the other way, they hadn't been prepared for this kind of onslaught.

He had to find a way to get away from here, to get his treasure and run. Capture would mean death on the gallows, especially since he had murdered those Indians, including Sam Wolfkiller, before witnesses at the train station. A stupid move that had been, made under the influence of that wild, impulsive urge that always seized him in the midst of committing an armed crime. He didn't regret the killings, only the trouble they could mean for him.

Slidell went to another window and looked out. There

was one of the attackers, crouched behind a pile of logs. Slidell grinned as he took aim and laughed as he fired. The man took the slug in the side, tried to run away, then fell.

Slidell worked his rifle lever and laughed again, for tethered near the man he had just killed was a saddled horse. Slidell opened the door and made a run for the horse. His move was poorly timed. Around the corner came two more attackers. He wheeled, firing off a shot from hip level, and drove them back. He vaulted into the saddle from behind, jerked the tethers loose, and took off at a run.

One of the gunmen behind him stepped out, aimed carefully, and took a shot. Slidell cried out as a slug ripped through his shoulder. Blood poured down, front and back.

Slidell bent low in the saddle and rode as hard as he could, hoping he could make it away before he passed out.

At least he had his money.

Slidell, grunting with exertion and pain, pulled the dirty sack from the metal box in which it had been buried. He was in a rugged rocky area, two miles from the embattled ranch site. No one but he knew of this little rocky enclave, his own private stash for stolen money, goods, guns. He grinned as he plopped the money sack down before him. He dug into the metal box and removed a smaller bag containing the few stolen jewels he had not turned into cash. These he dropped into his pocket. Closing the box, he slid it back into its little cavern in the rocks and placed stones over the opening.

Exhaustion overwhelmed him, and pain rumbled through his shoulder. Slidell longed to lie down, even on these rocks, and sleep. Couldn't do it, though. Had to go on. At least he had his money. He slung the money bag over the saddle horn, mounted, and rode.

An hour later he jerked spasmodically in the saddle. He had gone to sleep and almost fallen. Turning, fighting the pain and weakness raging through him, he looked behind. Someone was back there, following him. He could sense a presence upon that wide landscape.

He felt cold and noted a north wind blowing. Eyes scanning upward, he saw a dense black cloud rolling across the sky like a coat of thick paint. The spring wind rode on its mantle. Between powerful gusts he felt the stickiness of humidity in the air, moisture driven all the way from the Gulf of Mexico far to the south. Thunder rumbled like a growling belly somewhere inside the dark cloud.

Slidell felt the wind, tasted the air, studied the squall line forming in the sky. He was a man of the flatlands and knew this sort of weather and what if often led to. The thought brought fear. He remembered a time in his boyhood when he had watched a house in his native Kentucky explode with his grandfather still inside. They had found him a day later, hanging ten feet off the ground, impaled on a sharp branch like a ham on a meat hook. He had been sucked into the sky and stuck on the tree when the swirling demon that had grabbed him finally tired of making him its toy. Ever since then, Caul Slidell had suffered a deep fear of tornadoes.

He pushed on, heart pounding like a hammer, his blood a dry crust on his shirt and coat. The wind continued to rise. He could feel the coming storm as he could feel the unseen presence behind him. He stopped and turned again, looking for his follower. The day was darkening. "That you, Jim Christmas?" he yelled. "Come on, damn your eyes, show yourself!"

No response but a peal of thunder.

A mile due north, Slidell recalled, was an old shack. If he pushed hard, maybe he could make it there before the storm hit and before Jim Christmas, if Christmas it was, caught up with him. He feared Jim Christmas even more than the cyclone.

Halfway to the shack he felt the presence again, more strongly, and twisted in the saddle. This time he saw him, starkly outlined against the purple-black sky. It wasn't Jim Christmas. For a moment that brought relief—then he looked more closely at the rider and felt a shudder of fear.

Cherokee Joe. He knew him even from this distance. The same Cherokee Joe who had ridden with him a time or two in the past and whom he had come to despise because he sensed him the better man. The same Cherokee Joe he had tried to frame for attempted murder back in the Indian Nations and the same Cherokee Joe whose father he had gunned down for the fun of it at the Guthrie railroad station.

Slidell's heart bolted to his throat. Panicking, he wheeled the horse and pushed hard toward the shack. The thunder pealed like cannonfire, and rain began, mixed with hail. Slidell didn't have to look back to know Cherokee Joe was matching his pace. He felt him like a hot breath on his neck. Through the storm he rode, battered by rain and hail. He hardly noticed the pain in his shoulder now; he felt too much fear to feel anything else.

There. The shack. Slidell spurred the horse as hard as he could. Then the horse's leg found a hole, and the animal fell. Slidell pitched forward.

When he sat up, he knew that time had passed. He had been stunned by the fall. His eyes swept the land, looking for the horse. It had galloped off. On the ground lay the money bag. It was empty, the last of the bills blowing out of it and sailing off into the wind. Slidell watched it a few moments and heard someone laughing aloud. He recognized the laugh a moment later: his own.

He stood. His shoulder was bleeding again. The wind was so strong, it threatened to blow him over. He heard a roaring that rose suddenly, like a train about to come over the rise. Wheeling, he saw a black cyclone descend and etch a scar across the land, the shack that had been his goal in its path. It exploded before his eyes as if a bomb had been set off inside. Slidell screamed and threw himself into a ravine, clung to the brush in it, and heard himself laughing again. Death had come to claim him the same way it had claimed his grandfather, and he had cheated it, cheated it because of a fall from a horse.

He passed out again, and when he awoke, the cyclone was past. The wind had declined significantly, and the clouds were not as thick. The raindrops were just drops again, not bullets.

He sat up, groaning, then looked up and saw Cherokee Joe staring down at him. A peculiar gurgling sound rose from his throat. He dug for his gun and found the holster empty. Cherokee Joe lifted his hand. Slidell's pistol dangled from his forefinger.

"You killed my father, Caul Slidell," said Cherokee Joe.

"Joe, I didn't mean to do it, I swear, and it wasn't me—it was Wiltflower."

Cherokee Joe shook his head. "It was you, Slidell. Confess it!"

Slidell had no will to defy the halfbreed. Weakly he nodded.

Joe Wolfkiller flipped the pistol in his hand and aimed it at Slidell's head. The outlaw began to cry. He squeezed his eyes closed.

Click.

The hammer had clacked into an empty cylinder. God help me, Slidell thought, he's going to toy with me before he kills me. Going to toy with me like that Kentucky twister toyed with my grandfather.

The cylinder turned with a clean metallic whir.

Click.

Slidell sank to the ground, putting his hands over his face. Another whir.

Click.

"Please, Joe, please," he pleaded. "If you're going to kill me, then kill me!"

Click.

"Please, Joe. Don't play this game with me. Don't make me wait for—"

Click.

A long pause followed. Slidell knew the time had come. Cherokee Joe had reached the last shot. This time the sound of the turning cylinder was not a whir but a slow ratcheting.

Cherokee Joe spoke. "The first five were for the sake of a crazy old Indian named Will Ax who told me that those who won't bend will break, and that sometimes a man has to let himself forget, and that maybe the old ways of revenge are dead. And they were for the sake of an old widow woman in Great Bend who gave me a second chance and told me to make good of it—and for a Cherokee girl who wouldn't turn her back on her own kind, even though she could have."

Joe squatted by the ravine and aimed the pistol

carefully at Slidell's head. "But this last one—this is for the sake of Sam Wolfkiller, but mostly for the sake of Cherokee Joe."

Slidell couldn't keep his eyes closed for some reason. He found himself compelled to stare into the grim face above him and the hole of the pistol muzzle only two feet from his face.

"Joe, please. I'll make it worth your while if you won't—"

Click.

Empty. The last one was empty too. Slidell put his hands to his face and sobbed.

Joe Wolfkiller stood and holstered the pistol. "Me and you, Slidell, we've got something in common. There's nothing but the noose ahead for both of us. It may come sooner, or it may come later, but it will come. Men like you and me live short lives. That's all right. That's how it ought to be. We haven't earned the right to anything better.

"I've lived close to death these last days, and I've lived close to life. Now I know which is best, even though the knowing's come too late to count for much. The time I have left before they finally catch me will be short, but I'll have the satisfaction of knowing that one time, just one time, Cherokee Joe knew what it was like to forgive someone who wronged him."

Joe Wolfkiller turned and walked away through the rain. Slidell, his voice tight, stood. He gripped his wounded shoulder. "Cherokee Joe!" he called.

Joe turned.

"Why?"

Cherokee Joe looked him in the eye. "Because Will Ax was right. The old ways are past," he said. "The law of blood has faded. The *ulunsuti* no longer shines."

He turned again and strode away, long strides across the sodden, storm-ravaged land until Caul Slidell was alone.

Afterword

C*herokee Joe* was written under the inspiration of two events. The first was a drive from Wichita to Oklahoma City on a pleasant day in the summer of 1990, during which the impulse to write a story set in that beautiful portion of the Midwest became overwhelming. The second was reading in James Mooney's classic collections, "Myths of the Cherokee," and "Sacred Formulas of the Cherokees."

Among the subjects Mooney explored was the legendary Uktena, a large, serpentine creature said to haunt hidden pools in the mysterious mountains of western North Carolina, particularly the gorge of Nantahala. The dragonlike Uktena was said to have a brilliant crystal crest on its brow. This, the *ulunsuti*, was the rarest and most desirable of Cherokee divining stones, and was believed to give much power to its possessor. Mooney recorded that one *ulunsuti* was said to remain in possession of the Eastern Cherokees as late as 1890, but was kept hidden in a cave by a hunter who staunchly refused to desecrate and likely ruin the crystal by allowing any white man to look at it.

Several references to legends of the Uktena and the *ulunsuti* exist in early sources, including the recollections of Henry Timberlake and James Adair, both of whom lived and traveled among the Native Americans of the Southeast in the 18th century. Examination of this and other lore of the period is a rewarding effort highly recommended to interested readers, who may wish to compare the Cherokee stories with the similar legends of dragons and great serpents that abound across the globe.

One unrelated and final note is in order: The towns of Hutchinson and Great Bend, Kansas, are, of course, well-known actual locales. In *Cherokee Joe*, however, these towns are given a substantially fictional treatment. No characters presented in association with them (whether townsmen or local law enforcement officials) are intended to depict or represent any actual figures out of the histories of those communities.

CAMERON JUDD
July 15, 1991

If you enjoyed CHEROKEE JOE
by CAMERON JUDD, be sure to look for
his next novel for Bantam,

THE BORDER
MEN

Here is an exciting preview of this new Frontier
novel, to be published in May 1992.
It will be available wherever Bantam titles
are sold.

Turn the page for a sample of
THE BORDER MEN
by Cameron Judd.

She awakened swiftly, as was her way. There was rarely a twilight interim between sleep and alertness; she passed from slumber to wakefulness not like a diver rising through water, but like a hawk bolting from forest to sky.

Her name was Ayasta, and she lay in a log hut in the mile-long town called Chickamauga. Rising now on this early autumn night in 1778, she cast aside her blanket and walked silently across the packed dirt floor to the place where her son of three years, Wasi, stirred and cried.

He sat up as she reached him; his arms stretched out, and she embraced him. His thin body, afflicted again with the intermittent fever that had plagued him for the past two days, was hot against her breast. She could feel it even through her long linsey-woolsey shirt, which had been taken in some raid against a white farmstead to the northeast and given to her by Atsina, her elderly neighbor.

Atsina gave Ayasta many such gifts; the old woman's desire to goad the young widow into marrying her son was so obvious, it sometimes made Ayasta laugh behind Atsina's back, not in mirth, but in mocking irony. Could Atsina really believe her plain, lazy son could replace the brave and handsome John Hawk, Ayasta's slain husband? In the year since John Hawk's death, Ayasta had been given five opportunities to take husbands superior to Atsina's son and had denied them all. None could match John Hawk, and it was Ayasta's conviction that to live lonely with her slain mate's memory was better than companionship with some inferior substitute. She and Wasi were fine alone.

Wasi snuggled against his mother and stopped whimpering. Ayasta gently patted his back and sang softly the lullaby that, according to the old storytellers, the mothers of the lost clan of the Ani-Tsaguhi sang in the days before they turned themselves from human beings into bears:

> Ha-mama, ha-mama, ha-mama, ha-
> mama, Uda-haleyi hi-lunnu, hi-lunnu,
> Uda-haleyi hi-lunna, hi-lunnu ...

Within a few minutes Wasi was asleep again, soothed by the soft and repetitious music. Ayasta laid him down gently and pulled his blanket halfway over him so that he could cover himself later if his fever heat turned to chill. After that she sat on her haunches for several minutes, looking at her son in the darkness, which was only slightly dispelled by the flicker of the fire. Her thoughts were solemn, deep, even unwelcome, but also unavoidable.

The slender young woman rose and walked silently to the door. Opening it, she looked out over the sleeping town of Chickamauga, named after the creek along which it had been built. For a town so relatively new, Chickamauga Town was large and still growing. The ranks of its populace were swollen almost daily by new defectors from the Overhill Cherokees, Ayasta's native people. Other newcomers included malcontent Creeks, Cherokees of the Middle and Lower Towns, and even many whites who sought safety from the violence of the great war being fought between the Americans and the English.

Chickamauga was the town of Dragging Canoe, unappeasable foe of the white settlers and mentor and guide of John Hawk in his last months of life. Ayasta had lived in Chickamauga almost a year now, yet it still wasn't home. Despite its size and relatively healthy state of supply by the British commissary, Chickamauga and the other allied towns around it had about them an indefinable feel of impermanence, or so it seemed to Ayasta. They were children's play-villages of reeds and sticks, doomed to be blown away in the next strong wind.

Why did she feel this way? She asked herself the question as she looked out over the dark town. There seemed no reason for her pessimism. Dragging Canoe, after all, was strong in his determination to keep his people's lands and even to regain those already lost through the acquiescence of the Overhill Cherokees from whom he had seceded. Every day, his fighting force grew. And the alliance with the British against the Americans remained firm. Chickamauga Town and the Chickamaugas, as Dragging Canoe's faction had come to be known, should hold fast and remain long.

But it won't be that way, she thought. I know it won't. How she knew it, Ayasta could not say, but she knew it. Danger was coming to the Chickamaugas, to their cabins, fields, and townhouses . . . and also to herself and, worst of all, to Wasi. This was the great fear that gnawed at her, making sleep slow to come and quick to depart. The confidence so many of her peers placed in the British was a plant with no root. If the tide of war turned, the British might abandon the Chickamaugas as they had already substantially abandoned the Overhill towns, which now suffered dire need. Ayasta knew that one factor driving many young Overhill warriors to the Chickamaugas was that most persuasive motivator—empty bellies.

Ayasta closed the door and sat down in the darkness, regretting the frenzied activity of her mind. Now she would surely not sleep for the rest of the night. She would remain awake until dawn, chilled by the shadow foreboding that only she could detect.

She had once cautiously revealed her premonition of doom to Atsina, only to hear it mocked. And her brother, Ulagu, who by custom would one day train Wasi in the ways of warriors, had similarly chided her when she had hinted her worries to him. After that she kept her fears private, and in so doing learned something: Fears, like cave mushrooms, grow bigger when chambered in the dark.

Wasi stirred again but did not awaken. Ayasta went to him and felt his brow. Cooler now. That was good. Perhaps tomorrow he would be well, though even if he was, he would probably fall ill again before another month passed. He was a sickly boy. The old women, when they thought Ayasta did not hear, whispered that Wasi was weak and plagued by the witches of this mystic river country and probably would not live to manhood. And Ulagu, Ayasta well knew, was concerned and perhaps embarrassed by Wasi's sickliness. It was Ulagu's hope that Wasi would grow to be what John Hawk had been: stronger, wiser, braver, better than his peers. Yet his sickly early childhood was not a promising start toward such an end.

Good, Ayasta thought with a surge of defiant satisfaction. Good. If Wasi is too sickly to be a mighty warrior, I am glad. His father was a mighty warrior, and he did what mighty warriors do: he died. I won't allow Wasi to die too. I'll not lose him like I lost John Hawk.

Closing her arms around herself, Ayasta strode about the cabin, thinking how Ulagu would deplore her thoughts tonight. John Hawk would have felt the same, if he were alive, and there again was the point: John Hawk wasn't alive. His warlike life had led him to an early death. And now Ayasta's brother was determined to see Wasi, who was all Ayasta had left of her husband, follow the bloody tracks of his father.

No. Ayasta gritted her teeth fiercely. No. Wasi would not follow a path of death but a path of life—if such a path existed. One think seemed certain: It could not be reached from the towns of the Chickamauga. If Ayasta was to find it, she would have to look at another place and seek the help of others. And she knew where the other place was and who the helpers would be.

She smiled softly, at peace now. The great war within her had calmed. When the right time came, she and Wasi would find that path of life she so wished for. There would surely be a price to pay in finding it, but no sacrifice was too great for Wasi's welfare, even the sacrifice of the only way of life she had ever known.

Ayasta put more wood on the fire, then returned to her blankets and lay down on her left side, her knees drawn up, her hand under her head. She did not seek sleep, having been too often frustrated when she did, but this time sleep sought her. When Ayasta closed her eyes, she did not open them again until morning.

The old frontiersman paused and leaned, panting, against a beech, his blood-mottled right hand clutching his wounded left side. Brown autumn-dry leaves that would cling to the tree until spring tickled his face in the night wind. More blood oozed between his fingers and dripped to the sodden thatch beneath his moccasins. Alphus Colter closed his eyes a few moments, praying for strength. He opened them again, saw ahead the dark wall of the stockade that bore his name, and was relieved.

Not much farther now. If he could only keep from fainting for a few minutes more, he could make it to his brother's cabin and live. If he passed out, he doubted he could rise again. He would bleed to death on the wet earth, and the Tory raider Elisha Brecht would have claimed one more victim.

"Keep moving," Alphus said aloud to himself. "Keep moving, by Joseph."

He took a breath, winced at the pain of his stab wound, and advanced, using his long rifle as a crutch. Emerging from the edge of the forest, he moved slowly to the empty stockade. He leaned against it and kept going, rounding the front and passing the big double gate. Now he could see the new cabin of Thomas Colter, standing where the more substantial log house of his own late son Gabriel had been until the Cherokees burned it two years ago. Thomas's shutters were closed, but a sliver of faint light shone between them. The light meant hope. Heartened, Alphus advanced a little faster.

At this moment Alphus was immensely grateful that his bachelor brother had come from North Carolina to resettle at Colter's Station. He had been in the settlement a mere five months, but already his presence had brightened the gloom that had often enshrouded Alphus since Gabriel's violent death. Now, if God was willing and his legs were strong. Thomas would save his older brother's life.

The distance to the cabin seemed triple what it really was. With every step Alphus felt his feet growing heavier and his head growing lighter. Flashes of light began swirling across his vision, and he had to lean hard on the rifle to keep from falling. The buttpiece of the long weapon mashed deeply into the damp earth, causing Alphus to leave behind a peculiar trail of sign: shortly spaced moccasin tracks interspersed with the oval depressions of the rifle butt along with great spots of fresh blood every foot or so.

At the end, Alphus began to believe he would not make it. Thomas's cabin was only yards away and stubbornly refused to draw any closer. His vision swam and his legs grew weaker.

Only one thought kept him from falling, and that was that he was unwilling to die at the hands of Elisha Brecht. There were many men Alphus Colter would find no dishonor in being killed by. Brecht was not one of them. It wasn't solely because Brecht was the most hated and merciless Tory plaguing the American patriot frontiersmen. It was far more personal than that for Alphus Colter. The Colters and Brechts had been at odds long before either family crossed the mountains to this frontier, and Alphus had vowed that no Brecht would ever lay him low. Death at the hands of an honorable enemy Alphus could accept, if he had to; death at the hands of a Brecht he could not.

"Thomas!" he shouted feebly as he forced one more step out of his weary body. "Thomas!"

No sign indicated he had been heard. Tears began streaming down Alphus Colter's face, not drawn by fear or grief, but by exertion. "Thomas!" he shouted again. "Help me, Thomas!"

He advanced another ten steps before white light rose from the back of his eyes and obliterated his vision. He fell down but had the paradoxical sensation of rising at the same time. The ground slammed against him like the palm of a great slapping hand.

"Thomas..." This time he could not shout, only murmur. The light in his vision began to fade and in moments was black.

"It was Brecht—you're sure?"

"That's what Alphus told me," said Thomas Colter. His face was still flushed from the exertion of his ride to Joshua and Darcy Colter's new home on Great Lime-stone Creek about a mile from where it spilled into the Nolichucky. "Please, Joshua—we must hurry!"

Sina Colter, the lean, weathered wife of Alphus, stepped forward and gripped Thomas's arm. As irony would have it, she had been visiting Joshua's cabin this evening, helping tend to Joshua's little son William while Darcy lay ill with a fever. "I'm coming too," Sina said.

"No, Sina," Joshua said firmly. "Stay here, and come in the morning. Too many people will slow us . . . and Brecht may yet be about."

"I'll not stay behind when Alphus needs me!"

"You will!" Joshua shouted in her face. She wilted back, looking tired, frightened, and as old as Alphus, though she was many years younger than her husband. Joshua regretted his loss of temper. "I'm sorry. It's what I think best."

She did not argue further. She withdrew to the fireside and sat down on a three-legged stool, wrapping her thin arms around her middle and gazing into the fire. Zachariah, Sina's nine-year-old son by her previous marriage to the late Levi Hampton, went to her and put his arm across her shoulder, manfully trying to be calm and brave but looking scared. The child had been born in the waning days of Sina's childbearing years and was her greatest comfort as the foreshadows of her declining years loomed.

The pale-faced Darcy, clad in a long homespun nightgown, went to her husband and kissed his bearded cheek. Her face was hot against him. "Be careful, dear heart," she said. "Watch out for Brecht."

"I will, Darcy."

The front door opened and Cooper Haverly entered. He was damp. The rain had resumed, a foggy drizzle. Despite their differing surnames, Cooper and Joshua were brothers by birth. Cooper had been born eighteen years before to their mutual mother, Hester Byrum, who had died bringing him into the world within the walls of a doomed English fort named Loudoun, and named Samuel by Joshua himself. He had been raised through unusual circumstances by a would-be frontier empire builder Peter Haverly. It was Peter Haverly who had begun calling his adoptive son Cooper, a nickname that had stuck harder than the boy's Christian name.

Cooper's path had diverged from Joshua's for many years, only to rejoin it here in this transmountain frontier. Difficulties and differences they had known in their day. Now time had healed old hurts, and they were again the brothers nature had intended them to be.

"The horses are ready, Joshua," Cooper said. "What do you want me to do now?"

"I fear you'll have no sleep tonight, Cooper. Callum McSwain came by today, heading down to get whiskey at Dudley Grubbins and Jim Birdwell's place. He likely put up there for the night. Go fetch him and the others, if they're not drunk, then roust out all the other rangers you can who can get to Thomas's cabin by sunrise. Maybe we can pick up Brecht's spoor in the morning and have him done for once and for all."

Cooper turned to leave; Joshua grasped his shoulder. "Be careful—I don't want you mistaken for a Tory raider and shot."

"I'll take care." And then he was gone. Moments later, the sound of his horse's hoofbeats receded.

"Let's be off, Thomas," said Joshua.

They rode in silence, swiftly following a trail that the horses knew well. Joshua was in turmoil as he prayed for the welfare of his wounded foster father. As bitter anger at the despised Elisha Brecht flared in him, he deliberately tried to quell it, for Joshua Colter knew that uncontrolled rage made a man careless—and where Brecht was involved, carelessness couldn't be afforded.

He had sensed that something was wrong the moment Thomas Colter pounded on his door. The white-haired merchant had rushed into the cabin the moment the door opened, almost spilling Joshua over in the process. "It's Alphus," he said., "Cut and near drained of blood—I heard his noise and found him in the yard. Come quick! Come quick and help him!"

Joshua urged more speed from his horse. A damp maple branch reaching down over the trail slapped his face in the darkness and swept off his broad-brimmed felt hat. He ignored it, leaving the hat behind and bending lower in his homemade saddle.

Alphus mustn't die, he can't die, not like this. He's the only real father I've known. God above, don't let him die on me now.

Joshua's thoughts raced back across the years. He remembered his first sight of Alphus Colter back in a long hunters' little station camp cabin in 1760 when this country was unsettled wilderness. Joshua had been only a decade old at the time and had taken refuge in Alphus's station camp cabin after a remarkable solitary journey across the wilderness, fresh from captivity among the Overhill Cherokees. So long ago that seemed, yet the memory of Alphus as he had been in those days remained starkly clear.

Now Alphus was much older, just two years shy of seventy. It was a remarkable span of years in a trying land where a man was considered old at fifty-five. Alphus had already outlived most men born at his time. In all the years Joshua had known him, Alphus had seemed younger than his years. Yet of late there was no denying he was not the man he had been. Age had gripped him and now was beginning that vise-like squeeze that never loosens. Joshua feared that his father might be too old to survive the knifing Elisha Brecht had inflicted.

When at last the panting horses reached Colter's Station on Sinking Creek, Joshua dismounted before coming to a full stop. He raced to the door of Thomas's cabin and pushed it open, only to find himself staring down the muzzle of Alphus's rifle.

"By Joseph, son, I might have shot you!" Alphus declared. He grinned a grin that was as weak as his voice. The long rifle trembled down and fell to the dirt floor, and Alphus lay back, closing his eyes. He was on Thomas's straw-tick bed, his head propped on a stack of rolled-up blankets. Joshua went to his side.

"How do you feel, Alphus?"

"How do you think? I'm weak as rainwater."

Joshua smiled, encouraged to detect a flicker of lingering feistiness in the wounded old man. It told him that his foster father would live. The thought brought such overwhelming relief that to Joshua's surprise, he began to cry. He leaned forward and put his arms around Alphus's shoulders, burying his face against his neck.

"By Joseph, boy, you're worse than a blubbery old woman," Alphus murmured.

THE LAND WAS THEIRS BY BLOOD AND SWEAT,
AND THEY STOOD TOGETHER AGAINST ANY-
ONE WHO TRIED TO DRIVE THEM OUT...

THE ARIZONA SAGA

by J. P. S. Brown

The Cowdens: Proud and independent, they drew
on their strengths of character, their old-
fashioned values, and their iron wills to survive in
a fierce land. Against the odds, this hard-fighting,
hard-loving clan rode tall in the face of danger,
determined to leave their brand on a land called
Arizona. Through three tumultuous generations,
this is the story of the Cowden century: the lives
and loves, the tragedies and triumphs of an
American family.

❏ **THE BLOODED STOCK**
28068-6 $4.50/$5.50 in Canada

❏ **THE HORSEMAN**
28562-9 $3.95/$4.95 in Canada

❏ **LADINO**
28979-9 $4.50/$5.50 in Canada
